Bone by Bone

a love story

Paula Martin

EARTH SONGS PRESS
www.earthsongspress.com

Earth Songs Press

BONE BY BONE: A LOVE STORY

Library of Congress Cataloging-in-Publication-Data has been applied for.

Cover Art:
Seventh Generation, 2017 (watercolor), Sophia Morell
Design by Carol Spencer Morris
www.cspencermorris.com

Printed in the United States of America
Print ISBN 978-0-9846199-9-3

for Annaliese, Sophia, and Jude

Bone by Bone

a love story

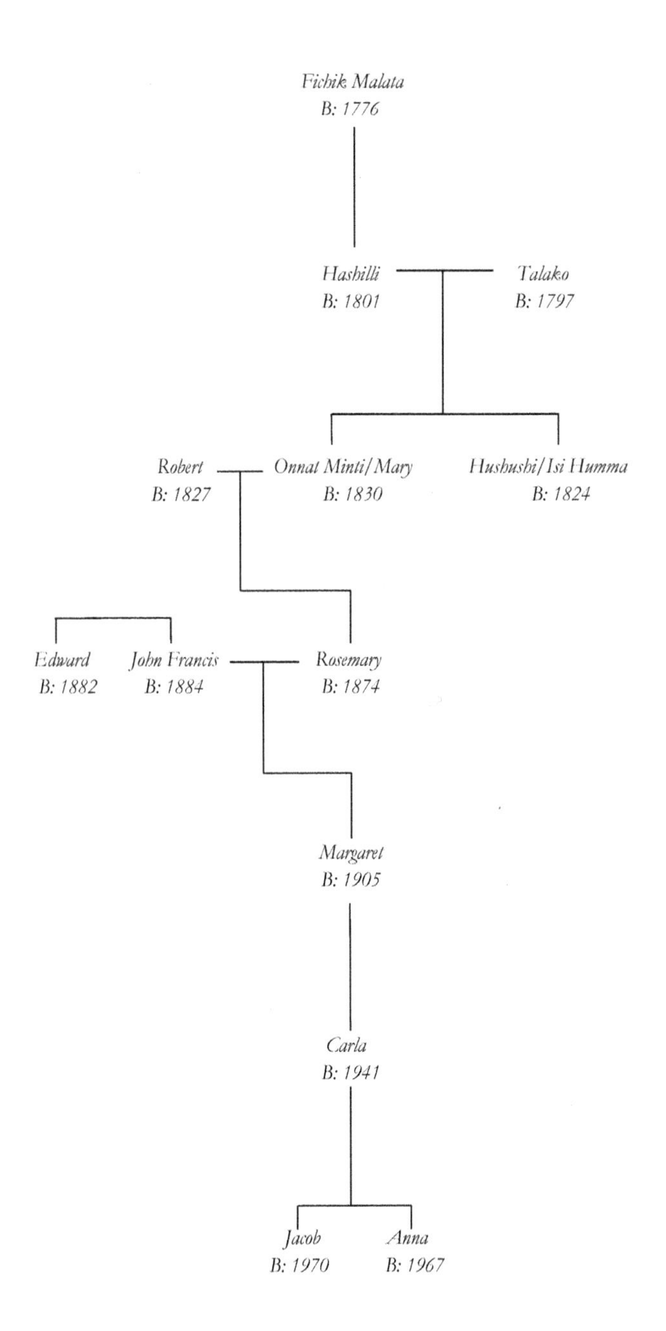
Fichik Malata
B: 1776
Hashilli
B: 1801
Talako
B: 1797
Robert
B: 1827
Onnat Minti/Mary
B: 1830
Hushushi/Isi Humma
B: 1824
Edward
B: 1882
John Francis
B: 1884
Rosemary
B: 1874
Margaret
B: 1905
Carla
B: 1941
Jacob
B: 1970
Anna
B: 1967

one

"There is no death. Only a change of worlds."

—Chief Seattle

Little Hunger Month, 1830

Old Choctaw Nation, Northwest Mississippi Territory

Talako stood ankle-deep in the river, the sand soft under his feet, his basket half-full with sleek, shiny fish. The knife his father had made for him as a boy was strapped to his upper arm. The sun, fulfilling its daily promise, rose slowly over the pines on the opposite bank as Hushushi, Talako's six-year-old son, played behind him at the base of a tree, its sun-bleached roots curled around him.

Talako took a deep breath, his bare chest filling with air, and prayed to the water to run up his veins, fill him with its spirit, and return back through his soles. He felt his cells come alive as the river flowed through him. Out of the corner of his eye he saw a blue heron flying upstream, gliding just over the surface of the water, graceful wings outstretched, yellow eyes unflinching. As the heron passed in front of him, a Great Horned Owl screeched from the shaded forest behind him.

He closed his eyes and bowed his head. This was the third morning in a row the owl had called to him at this time, three weeks after his daughter had been born, three weeks after his people had been tricked into signing the treaty at the creek where the rabbits would never again dance. The government had decreed that he and his people, tens of thousands of them, had to move, leave the water, trees, and bones of their ancestors behind. After weeks of silence and prayer, he and his wife made the decision to stay with their children in their homeland. The owl had been stalking him ever since.

The caw of a crow snapped his eyes open. The heron was gone, the owl silent. Even Hushushi didn't make a sound behind him. The crow cawed again, this time louder and more aggressively, from the opposite riverbank. Talako felt his skin come alive. With the third caw he knew it had begun.

He turned to Hushushi and grabbed his arm.

"Go home. Now. Run home to your mother right now."

Hushushi's eyes filled with tears. Talako knelt down on one knee.

"You must go now, Hushushi. Run home quickly. Your mother needs you. She will know what to do. Remember this: this is your home. This is my home. I will always be here. Now go."

Talako stood and lifted his son by the arm. The well-worn path would lead him home. He pushed his son gently but firmly as three crows came soaring overhead and began cackling and cawing. Hushushi looked one last time as his father pointed to the crows and held his finger over his own mouth. Hushushi turned and started running down the path toward home.

The boy could barely see anything through his tears. There were now so many crows in front of him it felt like that's all the world was. He knew they were telling him to follow. They became insistent, the whoosh scaring him as they dove and swooped, practically hitting him with their shiny black wings, leading him home.

The gunshot splintered the air over the river like glass, shattering it into a thousand pieces. Hushushi froze, the ringing in his ears drowning out everything, even the cawing of the crows. He pressed his palms against his ears, trying to stop time. Then the ringing stopped, and the world went silent. He looked down to see a red snake slither across the path just in front of him.

The silence broke as the crows' screams ripped through the air. Sleek, feathered wings dove and swooped, black beaks slicing the air behind him. Suddenly the crows' shrieks formed into words.

Run, they screeched at him.

Run.

Hushushi's bare feet beat the dirt trail like a drum as he ran as fast as he could, crows screaming behind him. He realized that he could see further than he ever could before, as if he could see all the way to his one-room house, as if he could see into the moment that hadn't yet come. His mother stood several yards from the front door, breathless, her eyes wild. His sister, just a few weeks old, slept against his mother's chest, her cheek pressed against her mother's soft skin, pursed lips facing upwards.

Hushushi burst out of the forest and into the clearing. His mother was steps from him when she grabbed his hand and they kept running, past the house, past the tan horse, up the jagged trail, the river and sun at their backs. The crows were now silent, the trees sheltering Hushushi and his mother as they disappeared into the thick green. Everything became shades of shadows. Even the squirrels stopped their chattering as he followed his mother, her long, black hair fanning across her glistening back, her bare feet bounding up the trail like a deer.

After twisting and turning up and up, they came to an overhang, and his mother ducked into a hidden cave. Hushushi stopped, his fear holding him back like a giant hand. He couldn't go in. He was dizzy, confused. He stood on the edge of time and space, a ledge that he could see over but his six-year-old mind couldn't comprehend. Then he realized why. He was in his dream, the one he had woken from a dozen times, standing at this very place, his mouth open in a silent scream.

His mother's hand reached out of the darkness and grabbed his arm. Her pull was gentle yet firm. The darkness enveloped them and Hushushi gave in, grasping his mother's arm with both hands. She led them along the wall until the opening was just a circle of light, a far-away moon. He felt her release, her whole body relaxing to the floor, and sensed the baby shifting on her chest. Then, the murmur of suckling. He curled into his mother against the cool rock wall and silently cried until he fell into an inky black sleep.

The circle of daylight at the cave's entrance was gone when Hushushi awoke. He felt his mother and sister's heartbeats in the darkness, soundwaves vibrating outward. He thought he heard a dull fluttering sound from deep within the cave, and in an instant his mother grabbed the side of his head and pulled him into her breast, curling her body over him and his sister just as a thousand leathery wings frantically raced over them toward the open night sky.

∞ ∞ ∞

The moon was huge, glowing, lighting the path as they silently made their way back down the way they came. Even the stars seemed brighter, as if they were shining just for them. About halfway down the jagged path Hushushi began to smell the familiar odor of smoke. Wait, what was going on? Had he fallen asleep and had a bad dream? Was his father at their house, sitting by the fire, waiting for them? Hushushi quickened his pace, his hands pressing gently on the small of his mother's back as they neared the clearing. She did not speed up.

A line of white smoke curled up from their small house, but it was not from their firepit. It was coming from the roof itself. The horse was gone, the door smashed off its hinges, the chairs his father had carved just broken pieces scattered around the yard. Hushushi looked up to his mother's face, but she kept her eyes straight ahead. The baby was breathing light and quick; he realized she had yet to make a sound since the crows led him home.

His mother quickened her pace when the dirt turned to sand. The water began to sing to them as their feet slid down the embankment. A smell surrounded them, not a smell, really, but something now part of the air they breathed, something sweet, ancient, and strangely familiar. And that's when they saw him.

Talako lay face-up, the moon reflecting off his skin, his head cradled by the bleached roots Hushushi had been playing in just hours before. The sand around and under him was stained dark red. Hushushi couldn't take his eyes off the hole in his father's chest. It felt like he could see inside his father, and his father was looking through that hole right back at him. His mother fell to her knees and started rocking back and forth, pulling her hair with both hands.

A moaning, guttural sound started so low Hushushi didn't even hear it at first. But then his skin prickled and his senses went into high alert. Before long it was getting louder, and closer, and Hushushi realized it could be a panther coming to clean his father's bones. His hand trembled as he reached to touch his mother's back, but then she turned and locked eyes on his. And it was her but not her, as if the face of a panther was moving across her face like a dream. And that's when he knew that it was his mother, not a panther, making that noise.

Then, as quickly as it started, it was over. Her face softened, there was silence, and she sat back on her heels and pulled Hushushi close.

She slowly untied the knife from Talako's arm and cut off a lock of his hair. Then she kissed his cheek, grabbed his ankles, and dragged him down to the water. Hushushi's mother spoke no words aloud as she pushed Talako into the river, but Hushushi could feel the silent prayers in the air like twirls of smoke. She then stepped back and knelt in the soft, brown sand and sang soundlessly.

Talako floated for a moment as the current took him downstream, then he was gone. Hushushi wanted to jump in after him, let the river take him, too. His mother must have felt his thoughts because she stood, walked over to him, and pulled him down on her lap beside his sister. Then his mother signaled to Hushushi to look out over the river.

The moonlight glowed on the flowing water. Something small rustled in the grass, the baby cooed. Then, right in the middle of the liquid reflection, a huge fish jumped, its scales glistening in the moonlight. As it splashed back in the water another fish jumped, then another, and another. Hushushi's mother began to giggle quietly, and then he did, too, as hundreds of fish jumped and splashed, the river singing, the moon glowing. Out of the darkness an owl flew over, his silent wings dropping a feather on the sand in front of them.

Hushushi didn't know how long they sat there on the river's edge, the fish twirling and dancing, his mother's joy permeating his skin. It could have been moments, it could have been lifetimes. But one thing Hushushi did know: what his father had meant that morning.

He would always be here. This was his home. He was home.

two

"Men must be born and reborn to belong. Their bodies must be formed of the dust of their forefathers' bones."

—Chief Luther Standing Bear

November 30, 1831
Arkansas Post

Fichik Malata carefully stepped off the *Reindeer* as she clasped daughter Hashilli's outstretched hand, their bare feet sinking into the cold, muddy riverbank. It was well after sunset, and two thousand of their people were crammed onto three steamboats that had made their way from Vicksburg up the strong, swirling Mississippi River, then a short journey up the Arkansas River to this stop. The soldiers had told them that they would need to get off here at this dark, swampy place, but they weren't saying why. Fichik Malata's stomach quivered when she realized that the river water, which usually sang the ancient songs, had become silent.

The wind was cold, much colder than it should have been, and the few blankets on the boats had gone to the children and elders. She had given her blanket to a crying woman cradling an infant. As the woman thanked her, out of the corner of her eye Fichik Malata saw Hashilli shiver, and she knew she was thinking of her own children, Onnat Minti and Hushushi, back in their homeland. At only one and seven years old, Fichik Malata's grandchildren wouldn't be strong enough to make the journey in the winter. She and Hashilli had wanted to wait until the next summer to follow the orders to leave their home, but the agents wouldn't let them. Fichik Malata's older daughter's husband had been one of the few hundred who had signed up to be able to stay, so she had urged Hashilli to leave her children with her sister until she could send for them. It had been two weeks since they kissed them goodbye on the dirt road.

She stood beside her daughter and quietly watched as their people stepped off the steamboats by torchlight, one by one.

It didn't take long for word to spread that there were

only sixty tents, and the soldiers took half of those. Thankfully, the ground was not yet frozen, and Hashilli was able to gather enough pine needles to make a soft spot for the two of them to curl up into each other and sleep. Her dreams were liquid, watery, a leaf haphazardly swirling downstream.

Morning came cold and dreary. Fichik Malata saw that the steamboats they had arrived on were gone, and as she raised up she saw hundreds of groups of people gathered around small fires, warming their hands and feet. Hashilli had joined a group from their town. It was a strange feeling, to be on land. The cold ground felt stationary, solid. She couldn't quite shake the feeling of dread that kept wanting to wrap around her like a soldier's wool coat. But she knew better than to succumb to fear or doubt. This was the way she had been shown.

She joined her daughter at the fire and allowed it to slowly coax the feeling back to her fingers and toes. Talk was cautious, low. An elder had coughed all night, children were hungry. Fichik Malata felt Hashilli looking at her to see what to do next. Without looking back, Fichik Malata nodded slightly. Then she began to walk.

Her daughter followed as Fichik Malata wove her way through their people, then across the field to the river's edge. She lifted her long skirt mid-calf and stepped into the frigid water ankle-deep. Both of her children had started life by a river, the same one where her son-in-law had lost his. And though Fichik Malata had never been at this particular place, she knew this water. She knew all water. It was all the same, connecting the rocks and the mountains, the past and the future, her and her mother, her and her daughter.

Fichik Malata closed her eyes and began to quietly sing to the river, her soles sinking into the silt. The crackling of the fires, the occasional barking of the soldiers, and the scared, hushed voices of her people swirled downstream and faded away as Hashilli joined her in softly singing. At some point she felt her daughter's firm hand clasp hers. Far away at first, and then closer and closer, she began to hear the faint murmuring of the songs echoing back to her from upstream. She breathed deeply and let them roll through her in waves.

When the singing became as constant as the air she breathed, she opened her eyes. She looked to her daughter, whose eyes were still closed and who was now silent, but who was vibrating like the red of a cardinal's wing. And for the first time she knew that Hashilli had reached the silence of the center, and that she would know when it was time to know. She squeezed her daughter's hand, and then they both turned and walked up the muddy riverbank to join the others.

The sun finally came out that afternoon, but its appearance was brief. After that, the north wind blew colder and colder. By day three the soldiers had rationed food to one handful of parched corn, one turnip, and two cups of hot water per day. Children's cries kept her up at night, and the wailing of women haunted her during the day. Then the snows came and froze the pine needles, mud, and bare branches. The next day the snow continued and kept the fires from burning. The snow finally stopped, and Fichik Malata and her daughter spent the next two days singing softly and watching the bend where the ships would soon return. Then, on the seventh day, news of the river freezing spread like wildfire from campfire to campfire.

The ships could not return. The wagons couldn't get to them. They were on their own.

That night the stars shone like a newborn's eyes. With so many children and elders dying the past few days, Fichik Malata was able to get a blanket, but even then it barely covered her small frame. The last thing Hashilli remembered that night was the soft, wrinkled skin of her mother's neck as she held her on her lap like a child and sang as the fire died down to glowing embers.

When Hashilli opened her eyes the next morning, pinks and purples filled the sky like a child's laughter. The sun was finally coming out again. She felt warmer than she had in days, and as she shifted on the frozen ground she realized that she was covered in a blanket. Her mother's blanket.

And she was alone.

Hashilli sat up quickly, the blanket pooling around her waist. The smoke from a dozen early fires rose up like prayers around her as her eyes darted around, searching. She stood up quickly on stiff legs as the blanket fell to the ground. She picked it up and stumbled toward the closest fire.

After desperately searching faces by the third fire she began to run. Her numb feet slipped on the ice, and she couldn't feel her hands hit the ground. Her cheek smashed against the ice, and she lay there, hot tears finally releasing. Then she heard the river's song.

She slowly lifted her head and looked across the field toward the water. The field was soft white like a cloud. Hashilli was suddenly three years old, and her mother picked berries beside her as she lay on her back on the grass and stared at the tufts of clouds floating by. Her mother's purple juice-stained fingers reached out and touched Hashilli's cheek, leaving her fingerprints there. Hashilli giggled and grabbed her mother's hand in her small one.

The cold wind stung her cheek and brought her back to the frozen field. And that's when she saw her.

Hashilli stood up slowly and wiped the blood from her cheek. Her eyes never left her mother. She could no longer feel the frigid wind blowing through her clothing, but she wrapped the blanket around herself anyway. And she began to walk.

She found her mother's footprints and placed her own feet in each one. The world went more and more silent with each step. The sky was now a brighter blue than Hashilli could ever remember, the sun lighting up all of the corners.

Her mother lay curled up on her side in the middle of the field facing the river, her long grey braid curving on the snow like a snake. For a split second Hashilli allowed the thought that she was just sleeping to enter her like a dream, but then she knelt down in front of her mother and saw the ice glimmering on her lips, nose, and eyelashes. Her eyes were open, her skin almost translucent. She looked innocent, unafraid, as if she had already forgotten the pain of living. As if she were a child again.

Hashilli felt panic surge through her and unground her. She had to get her mother back to her birthplace to complete the circle of becoming the soil, the leaves, the berries. Like her own mother. And hers. And hers.

Hashilli stood up on the slippery ground, grabbed her mother's arm, and tried to yank her up. Her feet kept slipping as she pulled, fell, got back up, and pulled. But her mother wouldn't budge.

She was frozen to the earth.

Out of breath and aching, Hashilli collapsed. The world once again went silent as she allowed the tears to come. When she could no longer feel anything, she sat up, gently lay the blanket around her mother, and then crawled under it into the crook of her mother's body.

In the darkness she closed her eyes and watched as the river songs turned into waves that picked her mother up and carried her back down the Arkansas

River, back down the Mississippi River, then across the land and home. When the songs turned into an acorn that absorbed into Hashilli's heart, she knew.

She crawled out from her mother's arms, wrapped the blanket back around herself, and began making her way back toward the fires. Her eyes remained closed as she walked back the way she had come, step by step, in her mother's frozen footprints.

three

"Even the seasons form a great circle in their changing, and always come back again to where they were. The life of a man is a circle from childhood to childhood, and so it is in everything where power moves."

—Black Elk

January 05, 1832

North Little Rock, Arkansas

A myriad of stars lit up the night sky, glistening on the dusting of snow on the clearing like distant memories. Hashilli slowly sat up on the damp earth in front of the smoldering fire, a stack of firewood behind her, three women sleeping around the fire on her left, three on her right. Every bone, muscle, and fiber of her being ached for release from the agonizing pain. She felt the stars calling her, tempting her to untether from the earth and float away into their embrace. She sat up straighter, forced her eyes open wider. She was not ready to go. Not yet. The circle was not yet complete. Her children would not know where to go. She must make it to the land they had been promised, then send for them to join her. They were too young to try to find their own way.

Hashilli had a vague recollection of these same six women encircling her what felt like a lifetime ago as the soldiers lay her mother in the cold earth, the local preacher reading words she didn't understand from a brown leather book. There were so many bodies that there was only one grave, a huge hole in the back of the Frenchman's graveyard that had been dug by the nervous settlers and prayed over by the missionaries. A week later they were told they would have to walk the rest of the way to the treaty land.

Hashilli and the others still able to had been walking for ten days straight, stumbling along behind the wagons and horses, stopping only to sleep, and then up at the first sliver of daylight to continue marching west. Each step away from where she left her mother was a lifetime, each step away from her children back in their homeland an eternity.

When they set up camp this time, word spread that the next several days would be spent at this soggy encampment on the north bank of the Arkansas River, then they would cross the river and keep walking. The thought of that was almost unbearable.

Hashilli shifted on the cold ground, pulled her mother's blanket around her tighter, and gazed into the fire, now just a mound of dying embers. The night felt empty, alone. Out of the darkness a man coughed, a child whimpered. Hashilli's body stiffened against the sounds. She just couldn't feel any more suffering.

The remnants of wood glowed red and shifted in shadows like a breeze rippling across a meadow. Gradually her defenses melted, and she felt her breathing deepen and her vision soften. It was only a moment before the embers transformed into faces, and Hashilli watched as spirits and ancestors came and went in subtle flares: her grandmother, her mother, her father, her husband. Then her son as a man, her daughter as an old woman, five generations later a child with green eyes.

Hashilli allowed the sleeping breaths of her people to pass through her, opening her to the mystery of the darkness. She let her shoulders release as she breathed in the breaths of her people for the first time since leaving her homeland, her body relinquishing, her mind relaxing into the blackness of the void. Over the years she had had glimpses of what was coming, like when she sat by the riverside and held her dead husband's hand, but until this moment she didn't feel ready. But now, like a bear entering the cave for winter, she realized it was the darkness that would prepare the world for new life.

She sensed her ancestors in the cold wind around her, those who had come before and those who would come after. They lifted her up, and she felt no more pain as she stood and began to walk through the hundreds of people huddled together and sleeping. She walked toward the river to the edge of the encampment, and then saw a deer trail into the woods. Ancestors hummed around her like lightning bugs, tiny lanterns leading her forward.

As soon as she entered the cover of bare branches, she heard the river's song for the first time since she had left her mother's side. It flowed through her like water, beckoning her to let go completely. With instant clarity she knew everything in her life had led to this moment. There was no turning back.

Hashilli took two more steps, leaned forward, and placed her hands on the snow-dusted trail. Sleek black fur rippled down her skin as her body transformed and her hands and feet shifted into thick paws. Her silken whiskers were threadlike, her teeth thick and sharp. The night shone as bright as daylight through her fire-yellow eyes.

Her panther paws were silent as she padded down the deer trail, the ancestors merging into the air itself as she breathed them in and out, white vapor streaming from her nostrils. Up ahead she heard an oak calling to her, so she sped up, her powerful muscles rippling in waves. The stars shone overhead with the light of her ancestor's ancestors.

When she got to the old oak she stopped, her thick black tail swaying behind her. She took two steps, her tail brushing the gnarled trunk of the tree, and she knew the oak was telling her to look around. She saw she was in a clearing. Ahead and to the right stood another great oak, and ahead to the left, another. The three trees formed a triangle in the forest, and in the center the stars twinkled in the snow. She growled low, licked her muzzle, strode to the center, and stalked in a circle, clockwise.

When she completed one rotation she began to dig. Her great paws clawed into the earth, dark, moist dirt flying out behind her as the hole got deeper and deeper. Before long she was shoulder deep, then hip deep, and then the hole opened up to an underground tunnel and she sprang down. Deeper into the earth she bounded until she came to a ledge overlooking a smoldering campfire encircled by six sleeping women, a mirror image of the one aboveground at the encampment. Without hesitation, she sprang. As soon as she landed her fur absorbed into her skin as her bones restructured, and Hashilli stood upright and shook out her long, black hair.

The women slept soundlessly, the embers glowing. Hashilli blinked with moist eyes and looked around. She saw the roots of the three great trees intertwined, and passageways connecting them with each other. And she knew she was seeing what had been there all along.

Hashilli knelt down at the glowing remnants of the fire and began to blow. Fiery embers danced in red and orange as her breath brought them back to life. She blew harder. When a yellow flame erupted from the ashes, she reached behind her and added more wood to the fire. One woman shifted, another coughed lightly. The wood caught and huge flames licked and crackled.

Hashilli looked up to see that the earth above her

had opened up and a multitude of stars lit up the night sky, glistening on everything below them. The stars once again called to her, whispering to untether and float away into their embrace. This time she was ready.

She crouched down low, and then dove headfirst into the fire. Flames burst from orange to white, and Hashilli once again transformed, this time to pure white smoke. She rose past the earth's surface, lighter than air, swirling like a river running up, up, up. Below, the earth closed and she saw her empty body lying in the center of the clearing, a green sapling sprouting from the center of her chest. She continued to rise as her ancestors joined her and they spiraled up and up, higher and higher, until at last they reached the star-filled heavens.

four

"It is not necessary for eagles to be crows."

—Sitting Bull

October 18, 1858

Lafayette County, Mississippi

Isi Humma slipped behind an immense cypress tree, its trunk flaring out gracefully at the water's surface like a lady's skirt. His father's knife was strapped around his upper arm and he wore buckskin pants, a small pouch dangling from his side. His black hair lay in a shiny braid down the middle of his back. Their horses neighed and snorted on the other side of the ridge, but he knew the outsiders wouldn't come into the dark, damp swamp with her hissing snakes, screaming cats, and ghosts of those left to wander without a home. They never did.

He carefully stepped around knobby cypress knees and softly landed on the bank, soles sinking into mud. He was a shadow, one of the ghosts, slipping through the bends like mist. As he had been for the past twenty-two years.

He followed the well-worn path deep into the heart of the swamp. He breathed deeply, the horses and outsiders now far from his thoughts. The leaves were starting to turn yellow, and the first ones had begun to fall. The past few days he felt like pieces of himself were beginning to fall away, too, like clues left behind, though he didn't understand how or why. Sunlight streamed through the thick moss-covered trees, and for a moment he remembered another time and place when sunlight had filtered through a canopy of trees as he held his mother's hand and ran. His name was Hushushi then, his first name. But that name was erased after his father was murdered and his mother kissed him and his baby sister goodbye, tearfully hugged her sister, and whispered she would send for them soon. His mother running to catch up with the others walking was the last time he ever saw her.

When his aunt died three weeks later from the soldier's blanket, the missionary found him wandering toward town holding his sister. He was given the name Peter. The missionary's wife dressed his sister in her daughter's sleeping gown, then put him on a stagecoach to the missionary school. He cried silently when they cut his hair. He couldn't understand how the missionaries would make him memorize the stories of Jesus, who kicked over the gold and healed the sick, yet would whip him with a switch when he was found outside in the forest surrounding the school.

The trail wound around to a one-room cabin backed up to a small pond that lay secluded in the cypress swamp. He wiped his feet on the straw mat outside his door. His cabin was sturdy, quiet. Off and on over the years he had shared the swamp with other ghosts, but he preferred to keep company with his own thoughts. The anger that had threatened to consume him as a young man was tamed long before, absorbed into his being like rain into the earth. He had no desire to hear news of the deception and suffering. from outside the swamp. He was at home with the silence of the dust of his ancestors' bones.

Once, many years before when he was eleven years old, eight days after he had slipped away from the missionaries at the stagecoach station and made his way into the swamp, he had gone past the ridge, stalking a small doe. He had been eating only berries for over a week, and he was dizzy with hunger. She kept coaxing him further and further out of the darkness, his hand clasping the blowgun he had made from the sugarcane reeds, darts carved with his father's knife. It had been four years since he had been in his homeland, much less hunting, but he remembered what his father had taught him. He crept out of the darkness, eyes locked on the doe as her ears flickered, his hand raising the blowgun to his lips. Suddenly she bounded off, white tail bobbing in tall grass. Before he realized it he was looking into a blond boy's pale face as it bobbed up and down inside a carriage. The boy looked to be about his age, and the boy saw him, of that he had no doubt. But he knew better than to make any sudden movements. He became a tree as the carriage rumbled past. The boy watched him until they disappeared from sight.

Not long after, his father's old friend, Hashuk Malli, found him huddled under a willow and unable to walk anymore. Hashuk Malli picked him up and carried him to the cabin. He didn't remember much about the next few days except for trembling sweats and freezing chills, wet leaves pressed on his forehead, thick liquid sliding down his throat. Smoke.

After that Hashuk Malli took him in. Hashuk Malli had been living in the swamp since the forced removals four years before, after his wife and daughter died in a fire. He was like a father in so many ways, and when he died ten years later, like Isi Humma's own father, Hashuk Malli became the wind, the water, the trees.

Isi Humma was reaching to push open the door when he stopped, his hand suspended in midair. He knew what it felt like to be watched by ghost eyes. Since Hashuk Malli's death, a handful of invisible ones like him had lived in the swamp, some of them coming out of the shadows to greet him, some not. This, however, was not the same. He turned around slowly.

A bald eagle sat high on a branch just a few yards to his left, his yellow eyes peering into his, unblinking. His yellow beak, the same color as his eyes, curved sharply, and Isi Humma could see the magnificent bird's talons as they gripped the wood. This eagle had been coming around a lot lately, watching him from first a distance, then easing his way closer and closer. Isi Humma slowly reached into the pouch around his waist and pulled out a small pinch of tobacco, bowed his head slightly to thank him for coming, and sprinkled the tobacco between them as an offering.

The eagle cocked his head to the side, fluttered his wings, and let out a shrill cry. Isi Humma felt the sound in his bones. He never broke his gaze as the eagle opened his massive wings. Two flaps and he was soaring just a few feet in front of him, two more flaps and he was rising clockwise, circling upward.

He watched as the eagle rose toward the sun, his spirals getting bigger and wider, as if Isi Humma was at the bottom of a great vortex. He could feel his spirit being pulled upward, and he instinctively knew that to resist was futile. Just as the fall gave way to winter, the time had come.

The sun was warm on his face as he breathed in and closed his eyes. He was the wind, the trees, the rocks, the moon. He was yesterday and tomorrow, a second and eternity. In his mind's eye he saw the eagle's wings encircling space and time and earth and spirit. He was everything and nothing at all.

When he opened his eyes again he was back in the shadowed swamp, his cabin behind him. The blue sky was now obscured by green leaves. An old buck stood on the trail in front of him, curled antlers reaching up like gnarled fingers. As Isi Humma got closer, the buck turned and trotted down the trail, beckoning him to follow.

Visions started forming in the tree trunks shadowed by slivers of light as he began to jog after the deer. His mother, bending at the waist, picking berries. His father stoking a fire with a birch stick. His sister, five years old in a white dress and hat, holding the missionary's wife's hand at the stagecoach station. Himself kneeling beside Hashuk Malli, head bowed in goodbye.

Vision after vision from his memories appeared around him as he ran after the buck toward the edge of the swamp. Sounds started echoing around him – the screech of an owl, the caw of a crow, the scream of a panther. He felt as though he was becoming less and less dense, that the water and space in his cells were expanding, opening the way. He felt lighter than he had ever felt in his life. As if he really was a ghost now, really was invisible.

Time stood still as the old buck stopped, looked back and snorted, then darted off to his right. Isi Humma stopped, too, his breathing heavy. The ridge loomed up ahead like a sleeping giant.

He didn't know how long he stood there, his feet reaching down into the earth like tendrils, connecting to all of the underground roots.

A horse neighed just as Isi Humma caught sight of the buck's antlers on top of the ridge. He felt himself being pulled out of the darkness. It was as if twenty-two years dissolved and he was again the scared, hungry boy who would rather die in the swamp than live in the outsiders' world.

But he was no longer a scared boy. He was a man now, a man whose unborn family would one day come searching for him, a man whose destiny was written into the stars. He knew he must follow his path.

Isi Humma sprinted up the ridge to the top. The old buck stood strong, his head straight ahead. Isi Humma heard the snorting of the horses and the hushed voices of the outsiders now, carrying through him on the wind.

He reached the top of the ridge and stood tall. For the first time since he entered the swamp as a boy, he let the sun shine down on him, lighting him from the inside out. He felt iridescent, like fish sparkling in the moonlight as he and his mother giggled, like shimmering stars. The eagle came soaring in front of him just as the rifle blasted, his yellow eye locking onto his, the light passing between them.

Isi Humma burst into a thousand butterflies, then

was inside of the eagle. He looked out of his new yellow eye, flapped his majestic wings, and glanced down as the old buck darted back down the ridge and into the swamp. He caught a current, soaring high above the outsiders walking toward the ridge. He circled higher and higher, wider and wider, spiraling around the treetops, the clouds, the sky. His mother and grandmother welcomed him with the songs of his childhood as he rose, and he let out a shrill cry as the stars joined in.

And then his wings grazed, and then became, the sun.

five

"When you see a new trail, or a footprint you do not know, follow it to the point of knowing."

—Uncheedah

June 06, 1890

Abbeville, Mississippi

A roll of thunder rumbled in the distance just as a fat raindrop plopped on Mary's shoulder. With her right hand she plucked several more yarrow flowers on her way up the walk and slipped them into her apron pocket, nestling them in with the rosemary sprigs and lavender buds. In sixty years, she had yet to find a man or woman to be as true as a plant. From deep in the woods beyond the cornfields she thought she heard the howling of the wolves, which she'd heard all her life. Since her mother's death the previous month, it had become more and more frequent. Mary quickened her pace as she made her way back up to the front porch just as the rain began to pour.

Once, when she was four years old, the summer sky opened up with rain and Mary stripped off her flowered dress and underpants and ran out the back door and down the steps. Her brother Jacob and sister Sarah laughed from the porch as Mary jumped in the puddles, dirty raindrops reversing their course. Sarah was pulling her dress over her head when their mother came stomping out the back door, eyes lit up like lightning.

"You know better than that, Sarah," she growled as she yanked Sarah's dress back down and grabbed her by the elbow. "You'd think Mary would know by now. Looks like the Lord has a lot more work for me to do."

The back door slammed shut behind Sarah, Jacob, and their mother just as thunder cracked. Mary jumped, her heart like a scared cricket in a jar, and then kept splashing and splashing.

Mary rubbed her feet on the mat and walked into the house she had shared with her husband Robert for thirty-four years. It was sturdy, spacious, surrounded by his family's cornfields. Robert's father had given it to them when they got married just before the War

Between the States. Even after all this time, she still felt like a guest. Over the years there were others filling the empty corners and hallways: Robert's sister Molly, Mary's mother, their five children. But no matter who was there, the loneliness still followed her around like a stray dog. Since her youngest and only daughter Rosemary got married last week at sixteen to a boy from a fine North Carolina family, the emptiness had threatened to consume her like a shadow overtaking a room, so Mary had spent most of her time outside in her garden. Today the rain had driven her back in.

Mary set her apron on the kitchen counter and poured water from the porcelain pitcher into the floral washing bowl. As the soap carried away the dark soil from her hands, a hummingbird darted by the window in a blur. Then it swung back around, dashed back to the window, and hung in midair right in front of her before taking off again.

Mary was suddenly five years old at the one-room clapboard church in Abbeville where her father had just been sent for his first true congregation. She, Jacob and Sarah sat stiffly on the hard, wooden pew, Mary's mother on her left. As their father preached about the Kingdom of Heaven, Mary's eyes ached, so she began looking around the room to try to keep them open. Sunlight streamed in through the window, and Mary's gaze followed it back through the plate glass and outside. A ruby-throated hummingbird floated just inches from the plate glass, emerald wings sparkling like a fairy's as she hovered in midair. She flitted up, then down, and side to side, as if she was talking to Mary, trying to tell her something. Mary felt a humming in her own chest as she relaxed and then rode the sunlight out the window like a stream of water. From outside the glass she watched herself giggling and watching herself dart and swoop on the other side.

Her mother's sharp elbow to her ribs and even sharper glare broke the spell, and Mary forced her eyes back to her father.

All these years later, she still yearned to be back on the other side of that glass.

Mary dried her hands on a kitchen towel and then walked to the bedroom that had been her mother's the past twenty-five years. On the bed sat a wooden trunk, the last thing of her mother's that she hadn't been through. Thunder rolled across the fields as Mary sat down on the bed and opened the lid.

Inside sat stacks and stacks of yellowed papers. Mary

picked one up and recognized her father's handwriting, and realized they were sermons that he must have given before he was shot outside Vicksburg while giving last rites to a soldier. She thought of her mother, about the age Mary was now, kneeling on his study floor placing page after page into this trunk, her once-black hair tied up neatly under her white bonnet, neck long and thin like a crane, dark eyes spilling with tears. When they had first moved to Abbeville, Mary had heard Mrs. Mason snarl, "Black Irish," under her breath when Mary and her mother walked by, then staring a little too long at Mary. That stare had stuck to Mary like mud, peering at her from behind a tree, following her through Old Man Chandler's store, watching her through white lace curtains. It had slowly dried and flaked off over the years, but there was still a shadow of ground-in dirt that remained.

Ten years later Mary sat at her desk in the one-room schoolhouse and felt the new boy Robert's blue eyes caressing the back of her neck. Eliza Mason kept whispering to Katy and looking back at Mary and snickering, and when Mrs. Smith left the room, Eliza leaned out into the aisle and said to Robert loudly, "You know Mary Wilson is just a dirty Injun, don't you?"

Jacob jumped up and told Eliza she better take that back as everyone started laughing, but Mary felt like she had been plunged under Crystal Springs headfirst. That night, when she asked her mother what Eliza meant, her father cleared his throat loudly and said, "It's time you told her, Nancy."

"We only wanted to save you, Mary," her mother had said, stroking her head. "God gave you to us so that you would be allowed into His Kingdom. Did you know President Jackson even had an Indian boy he saved when his parents died, just like you? You are a very lucky girl, Mary. I wouldn't pay any mind to Eliza Mason. You just stay quiet about this. No one needs to know. You just hold your pretty head high and know that you have a fine, loving family to take care of you."

Mary never spoke of it again, not even to Robert. When the tired census lady asked her race, she always said White.

Mary thumbed through a few more of her father's sermons, and then she came to a paper that was heavier than the others with ***Baptism*** in thick, bold letters at the top. Mary had already been through her father's church paperwork that her mother had saved before the church was burned in the War. Why would this be here?

Mary carefully pulled the paper out of the stack.

She shifted on the quilted bed and held the paper up. Under ***Baptism*** was *November 30, 1831*, and then:

Name: Onnat Minti

Christian Name: Mary

Mary's heart started fluttering like a hummingbird.

Parents: Talako (deceased)

Hashilli (removed to Indian Territory)

Mary forgot to breathe.

Finally, at the bottom of the page:

Adopted by Elijah and Nancy Wilson,

November 20, 1831.

Mary felt like forty-five years had washed away and she had again been plunged to the bottom of Crystal Springs. Images started forming on the shadowed wall: an endless line of starving women and children walking. Her sister-in-law Molly's Indian maid, head bowed. A train station, a rocky overhang. The jagged outline of a bat.

Mary sat on her mother's empty bed, in the shell of her house, and stared at the page. The word *removed* started vibrating, curling up at the pen strokes, and then turned into a bird and fluttered up and off the page. *Hashilli* followed, and then *Onnat Minti*, taking flight and circling around the room and finally out the window, one by one penetrating the glass and then following each other in a single line, forging a trail through the rain as they flew westward.

∞ ∞ ∞

That night Mary stood in the floor-to-ceiling window in a white cotton nightgown, her silver hair flowing down her shoulders, the June moonlight spilling across the grass like a dream. She quietly unlatched the window, opened it, and slipped out, shutting it gently behind her. The wood was cool under her bare feet as she made her way down the steps and onto the soil. Her nightgown puddled at her feet as she stepped out of it and kept walking.

When she reached the edge of the cornfield she stopped, lifted her face towards the sky, and spread her outstretched hands wide, palms up. She opened her mouth and the moonlight filled her as she drank it in like water. In the distance she heard the baying of the wolves, and she knew it was the same pack that had been stalking her all her life. For the first time she allowed their howling to absorb into her skin, awaken her remembering.

Mary closed her eyes and whispered her mother's name for the first time, *Hashilli*, the word rising from her lips like smoke. The wolves howled again, this time so close she could feel the heat of their breath against her cheek. Without opening her eyes she joined in with them, now part of the pack, their combined voices carried through time.

And then she let go, and became, the moon.

six

"They are not dead who live in the hearts they leave behind."

—Tuscarora Proverb

August 01, 1890

Spiro, Choctaw Nation, Indian Territory

The dream always started the same: mist floating on top of water, hovering just above the surface like a ghost. Robert is on the riverbank, his feet kicking the soft, brown sand as Mary waves to him from a boat out on the water. Years have melted away and they are smooth, unwrinkled, unencumbered by the weight of memories. Mary sits in the middle of the boat, white dress and parasol, balanced and graceful like a swan. Robert raises his hand to wave back, but as he does it feels thick, heavy, and he looks down to see that he is gripping a rifle and slowly bringing it up to his shoulder. Mary looks away for a moment, the wind rippling her black hair like waves as she reaches toward a heron gliding just over the surface of the water. Robert feels panic surging up his spine as the rifle presses on his shoulder and he screams her name, but no sound comes out. The barrel of the gun is long and grey as his eyes stare down it and his finger settles on the trigger. Mary's brown eyes sparkle and she reaches her hands toward him, holding the moment aloft like a bubble. The blast of the rifle shatters his ears and he smashes through the surface of the dream, eyes open, heart pounding, the scream lodged in his throat like a piece of meat.

∞ ∞ ∞

Robert glanced around the train car, a thin line of spit trailing from the corner of his mouth, his heart racing. If anyone noticed the old man jerking awake, they were ignoring him now. It was just as well; he didn't have anything to say to anyone. He just wanted to find Mary.

When she had boarded the train to Little Rock seven weeks earlier, she told him she would send a letter when she got settled at her sister Sarah's. Since her mother had died, she had been even more distant, so he thought her spending some time away might be a good change. She had spent her whole life in Abbeville, tending to him, their children, and then their grandchildren. The night before she left he had watched her from the crack in their bedroom door as she stared out the back window and quietly cried.

The day they married had been eerily charged, like the yellow air before a tornado. Two years later the ferocious winds of war would destroy everything in sight, but that day the future was just a distant uneasiness Robert swatted off his shoulder like a fly. Mary had been glowing, and even her sister Sarah's comment that Mary's dress was too tight rolled off Mary like dew. Her father was still alive then, and his voice bellowed through his white clapboard church. Her mother had sat firmly on the front row beside Sarah and dabbed the corners of her eyes. Sarah's eyes stayed dry.

After her mother's funeral, Robert had been walking back to lie down when he overheard Sarah say his name to Mary in the kitchen. He slowed down. "I think there's something wrong with him. It's not normal to constantly forget things. Why, he couldn't even remember today was Sunday. What kind of man doesn't know it's the Sabbath?"

"Oh, for goodness sake," Mary had said, her voice light like the wind. "Robert has never paid any mind to the little things. He's much better at remembering the big stuff, like which nights the moon will be full, what month the sun is the hottest, how much rain has fallen. I'm not worried about Robert and his memory. I'd be much more worried if he knew today was Sunday. Now that wouldn't be normal."

Sarah had huffed and hissed something under her breath. Robert had continued down the hallway, breathing Mary's words in through his nose in deep breaths.

The train whistled loudly, and Robert absently touched the breast pocket of his coat. When he got her letter two weeks after she left, he practically ripped open the envelope. She was at Sarah's, resting, and was planning to be there for a few weeks, maybe more. She was reading, going for long walks, watching the mockingbirds from the back porch. She asked him to not send her a letter yet, as it would be too hard to read what she was missing in Abbeville. He must wait until she sent him another letter before he responded.

When two more weeks passed and there was no letter for him at the post, Robert slipped on his glasses and wrote her about the long days and nights since she had been gone, how autumn was setting in, how the fields, and he, were tired. He almost didn't send it, but the next morning gave it to their newly married daughter Rosemary when she stopped by on her way into town.

Two weeks later Robert held a thick letter addressed to him from Sarah. His knees ached as he sat at the empty kitchen table and opened it.

Inside was his letter addressed to Mary, still sealed, along with a short note from Sarah in curt, staccato syllables:

Robert,

There must be some confusion. Mary isn't here. I haven't seen her since I had to come there for Mother's funeral in that dreadful heat. I talked with you and her then. Don't you remember? Rain hasn't stopped for weeks. Mother would have gone crazy.

Sending my love in Christ.
Sarah

Robert had pushed himself up from the table, his arms shaking. He felt like he was inside a bubble as he walked to their bedroom and picked up Mary's letter from his bedside table where he had set it every night for four weeks. There, staring back at him like a blue eye was the postmark: *September 01, 1890. Skullyville, CN.* It had been there all along, watching him as he slept. Robert sat heavily on the bed, creaks echoing down the hallway.

The screech of the brakes jolted him back to the train. He looked out the window as they pulled up to the Spiro station. There was a patch of woods off in the distance, and Robert saw a whitetail deer bounding toward the cover. He remembered a time over fifty years before when he watched from a carriage as a whitetail bounded out of the woods and Robert caught sight of a dark-haired boy about his age with dirt-covered feet and a sugarcane reed held up to his mouth standing still as a stone, only his eyes following Robert's. He thought maybe it was a mirage, or a reflection of an alternate version of himself, but with the memory of the last whipping he got for daydreaming still fresh, he didn't say a word to his mother beside him. He just kept his eyes on the boy as they rumbled by.

Robert shifted on the leather seat as the train slowed to a stop. The postmaster in Abbeville had looked at him with distant eyes when Robert showed him the postmark. He told him Skullyville used to be the center of the Choctaw Nation in Indian Territory, but after most of it was burned during the War folks started leaving, and when the train bypassed it a few years back and went a mile east to Spiro, Skullyville had become a virtual ghost town. It was just a matter of time before the post office there closed for good, he said. Only thing really left was the old Choctaw cemetery.

Robert carefully gathered his small bag and made his way to the exit. He would sleep in Spiro tonight, then at dawn walk the mile to Skullyville, to Mary. He remembered the hushed whispers about Mary. It was no wonder; she had worn mystery around her all her life like a shawl, as if she was hiding an ancient secret. Most people had been scared of it, but not Robert. He had been drawn to it like a moth to the light.

Robert stepped off the train and into the crowd of strangers. Maybe she had come here to find something. Maybe she had come here to find someone. Maybe, just maybe, after all these years, she had come here to find herself. He just hoped he wasn't too late.

∞ ∞ ∞

That night Robert's dream started the same: mist floating on top of water, hovering just above the surface like a ghost. He is on the riverbank, feet in soft brown sand, but this time there's no boat on the water. He is alone. Instead there is a campfire crackling behind him, and he turns and sits in front of it. Out of the corner of his eye he catches a flutter, so he looks to his right to see a white parasol rolling across the brown sand like a wheel. Mary. With a start he stands up. A heron floats by him just above the surface of the ground and over her dress, her hat, one white shoe. He hears his name behind him and turns back to the river to see her walking on top of the water toward him, her naked skin glistening in waves. Her bare feet step onto the sand and she walks up to him and grazes his chest with watery fingerprints. When he touches her waist, her body disintegrates into a pile of ashes. He hears her breath inside of him, whispering from the inside. "It's okay, Robert. It must be this way. How else will our great-great-granddaughter find me?" A gust of wind blows the ashes in swirls all around him, and he looks down to see a small white bone at his feet. Without hesitation he picks it up, walks to the river, and slides it into the water, the current picking it up and carrying it gently downstream in circles.

seven

"What is life? It is the flash of a firefly in the night. It is the breath of a buffalo in the wintertime. It is the little shadow which runs across the grass and loses itself in the sunset."

—Crowfoot

September 18, 1904

Abbeville, Mississippi

Rosemary peered around the drooping magnolia branch and watched as her husband William's hand brushed the curve of Betty's waist and the sixteen-year-old's cheeks flushed scarlet. A beam of sunlight streamed through the waxy leaves and down on the top of Rosemary's head, and she felt a bead of sweat trickle from behind her ear, roll down her neck, and absorb between her breasts. Today was her thirtieth birthday. That morning William had sighed disapprovingly as he tied the sash of her sea-green dress. "New dress or not, no wife of mine is going to flaunt her shoulders and chest in church. Go get your shawl and cover up." After church, Rosemary had left her fringed shawl on the back of the white folding chair as soon as William had left her sitting alone on the church lawn.

Rosemary watched as Catherine whispered into Betty's ear, gloved hands hiding giggles. She remembered being sixteen, her father walking her down the aisle, William's black suit punctuating the end like an exclamation point. "He's from a fine family," her grandmother had repeated that afternoon for the dozenth time as she sipped her iced tea, "wealthy farmers from North Carolina. He will provide you with a good life. You will never have to worry about a thing."

That night, Rosemary had silently cried as he sweated on top of her. When he rolled off and began snoring, she had slipped out of their bed and into her silk robe. The house was full of silent echoes, the ghosts of the children she was expected to produce running soundlessly down empty halls. She wanted to walk out the front door, down the long drive to the road, past white cotton trapped in rows and rows like tiny clouds, then start running, faster and faster until she ran up familiar steps and crawled into bed between her mother and father. Instead she had turned back toward the snoring and slowly made her way back to bed.

"Oh my, Miss Rosemary. You are looking flush. You ready to go on home?"

Millie was walking toward her, Rosemary's youngest boy Samuel on one hip, her white apron dotted with blueberry fingerprints. Millie had started working for them the day after the wedding and had been there for every meal, every holiday, the birth of all six boys.

Samuel looked at her through her father's sky-blue eyes and held out chubby, maroon-stained hands. Rosemary looked past Millie to see that both William and Betty were gone. Samuel scrambled up into her arms and pressed his face into her neck.

"Yes, I'm ready to go home."

Millie called to Willie Jr. and instructed him to keep up with his brothers and make sure they all made it home before supper. Rosemary nodded to the church ladies as she and Millie passed and they wished her a happy birthday. Rosemary couldn't tell if their eyes were sad for themselves or for her.

Samuel's breathing softened and became steady against her skin as the rhythm of her steps on the sidewalk lulled him to sleep. She ran her fingers through his light brown waves, just a shade lighter than her own, then brushed his petal-soft cheek with the back of her fingers. With each pregnancy she mourned her own death, but as soon as the pain split her open and she held her wriggling baby, slippery yet firm like a ripe pomegranate, she was born again.

"Wind is stirring up a spell, isn't she?"

The man's voice startled Rosemary and she instinctively covered Samuel's face with her hand and looked up. The flag on Chandler's Mercantile popped in the wind as several strands of her hair wrestled free. Two young men were stepping off the sidewalk as she and Millie walked toward them. The man who had spoken was in the front, hat in his hand, his chocolate-brown eyes bright with laughter. The man next to him stood with his eyes down, head bowed. Both men were tall with long, black ponytails and skin the reddish-brown color of the clay around Rosie's Spring.

"Stirring up something, sure enough, Edward," Millie grumbled as she sped up.

As Rosemary passed the man with his head bowed, she felt something drawing her toward him, a strong gravitational force, like the tide being pulled by the moon. When Millie's firm hand pressed into her lower back, Rosemary forced herself to look away, and the wind died back down.

"Who are those men?" Rosemary asked when they got out of earshot. It was harvest time, and hundreds of migrant workers were around, but she had never seen these men.

"That's the Littlefeather brothers," Millie said. Rosemary could feel Millie looking at her sideways as she spoke. "Cherokee boys. Confident one is Edward, his younger brother is John Francis. They joined Rufus' crew last week."

"Ah," Rosemary said, and then became quiet the rest of the way home. In the silence she saw her forgotten shawl dangling from the back of the white folding chair, the wind blowing the fringe like feathers.

∞ ∞ ∞

Three days later Rosemary stood in the dark, musty corner of Chandler's Mercantile fingering through bolts of fabric for some new curtains. Her back was to the door at the other end of walls stocked floor to ceiling with coffee beans, flour, oatmeal, molasses. The middle of the store was box upon box of soaps, elixirs, tobacco, and dried beans, with lanterns, pots and pans, rope, and ammunition perched randomly on top of overflowing tables. The silver bell tinkled almost continuously as farmers, wives, maids, and workers strode in empty-handed and out with full bags. George Chandler, Old Man Chandler's youngest son, stood behind the cash register answering questions and counting change at the same time.

Rosemary had just decided on the bright floral pattern and was turning to walk to the register when she stopped, her breath catching in her throat like a bird. There, standing just a few feet from her, was the man she had seen Sunday, John Francis, the younger one who had kept his eyes down. He stood on the other side of a table strewn with clothing, and Rosemary watched his long fingers tracing the seam on a pair of tan pants.

The door slammed loudly and Rosemary looked up, her hands gripping the floral fabric. John Francis was looking directly at her. Her heart fluttered as she tried to look away but couldn't, as if she were caught in an invisible net.

His eyes were inky black, even darker than hers, and his stare intense like burning coals. She felt herself drawn closer and closer, as if she was entering into them, and before she knew it time stopped, the world fell away, and she was floating in a sea of black, one light in a million sparkling, weightless stars swirling in a massive pinwheel.

Someone bumped her elbow from behind and the bolt of fabric clattered to the floor. She bent down to pick it up, and when she stood back up she watched his long, black braid as he made his way through the crowded room to the front door and out into the sunshine.

∞ ∞ ∞

It was cool Sunday morning when Rosemary walked barefoot down the trail to Rosie's Spring. She had said she didn't feel well and had Millie take the boys to church with William. It wasn't a complete lie. She didn't feel well, it was true, but she wasn't exactly sick. She just needed some time to herself.

Rosie's Spring was the largest of the cold-water spring-fed ponds on their land. The field workers cooled off there in the evenings, but they were all at church now. Rosemary had discovered it the first year of her marriage, stumbling with tear-blind eyes down the trail. That morning her sixty-five-year-old father had just boarded a train to try to find her mother, who had suddenly left him a couple of months before. Rosemary knew it then: she would never see either of them alive again. Until the day he died her father was convinced her mother would come back to him, so he moved into a house in an old deserted town on the other side of Fort Smith, Arkansas, where he was convinced she was, so that she could find him when she was ready.

Rosemary's Aunt Sarah had said that he had dementia and insisted Rosemary go get him and bring him back to Mississippi, but his letters were lucid, clear as the springs that ran through the rolling hills all around her, and she knew that making him leave would kill him. When Rosemary got the telegram five years later that he had died and wanted to be buried there, she had William pay for his Confederate Soldier headstone. Her mother never reappeared. All Rosemary felt was a hollowness when she allowed herself to think about her mother.

Rosemary quickened her pace as the trees got thicker and the green more lush. She didn't know why, but something about the clear, cold water made her feel connected, as if putting her feet in the water joined her with secrets, forgotten memories.

The path beneath her bare feet got softer and darker as it turned from dirt to clay. The bent tree at the curve pointed to the small rise that took her through thick vines and then opened up to the pond. A centuries-old cypress towered on the edge of the shore, its trunk flaring to over ten feet around at the base. Rosemary rested her hand against the bark as she stepped ankle-deep into the cold water.

She felt his gravitational pull before she saw him out of the corner of her eye. He was sitting on a rock on the edge of the pond a few yards down on her left. She kept her eyes on the water as John Francis stood and walked toward her. With each step he took, her grip on the past loosened. A frog croaked, a leaf landed soundlessly. When he stopped just inches from her, she knew that she had drawn him to this town, this place, this moment. And he had drawn her. They were both the moon and the tide, as old as the stars. The realization was unbearably fragile, like a pale blue robin's egg.

His lips were warm, his tongue salty like the distant memory of an ocean. Rosemary let go and allowed the waves to take her out to sea, one drop in a million of millions.

∞ ∞ ∞

Two weeks later Rosemary stood on the dirt road in front of her white-columned house, tufts of runaway cotton lining the sides as the orange sun slid toward the end of the road. He would be long gone now, following the planting, the harvests, the seasons. He had asked her to meet him at the train station at sunrise, said he would wait until the last train left that day just in case. She had promised him she would be there.

She pictured him and Edward sitting at the station, dark eyes searching faces, watching their backs as trains filled up to overflowing and then ambled away. The night before, Rufus had met her and John Francis at his and Millie's ramshackle house and told them that the whispers were slithering up to William like snakes and poisoning him with jealousy. Later, Rosemary tiptoed into her boys' rooms and buried her nose in their hair, one by one, as they slept.

The next morning she had awoken just before sunrise, quietly gotten dressed as William snored, and then pulled her packed suitcase out of the closet. Her hand had nervously smoothed the front of her skirt and then stopped on the soft space just below her navel. Waves of warm energy had radiated from her as something told her to unbutton her skirt and spread her palm on her skin. Her belly was alive, electric, like galaxies spiraling inside of her. And as clear as the water at Rosie's Spring, she knew.

New life was forming inside of her. A baby girl. John Francis's daughter.

The revelation had taken her breath away.

A few moments later when Millie had lightly knocked on the front door, Rosemary shakily told her to tell Rufus to go home. She would send for him later to take her to the station.

Rosemary had sat for hours staring at her suitcase, her doubts taunting her like a backstabbing friend. They would have nothing. She wouldn't see her boys. She was ten years older, and he would fall in love with someone his own age. Eventually, he would abandon them.

Only a sliver of sun curved over the end of the horizon now. It was orange and liquid, seeping into the end of the road. But Rosemary knew it was just an illusion; there is no end, she thought as she turned and headed up the long drive to her house. She saw the downstairs curtains part and her husband standing erect in the window.

She reached down and touched her belly.

Rosemary walked up the steps to her sprawling porch and turned and looked at the empty space where the sun no longer waited. It would be dark soon. Supper needed to be served, the boys needed to be tucked in, she needed to finish the floral curtains. She opened the front door as a crow cawed from a tree nearby, three others joining in from all four directions.

And another generation of seeds germinated just under the surface of the rich, dark soil.

eight

"We are earth people on a spiritual journey to the stars. Our quest, our earth walk, is to look within, to know who we are, to see that we are connected to all things, that there is no separation, only in the mind."

—Lakota Seer

October 10, 1918

Etienne, France

Private First Class John Francis Littlefeather felt the bullet streak through the side of his neck and out under his arm like a shooting star, leaving a trail of stardust in its wake. The dirt was unfamiliar under his back as he landed face-up, the memories of another man's ancestors embedded in the soil. Even though it was past midnight, the French sky was lit up as if it were noon. Somewhere close by he heard Edward scream his Cherokee name. The tat-tat-tat of machine gun fire surrounded him, like hundreds of woodpeckers drumming on hardwoods in the mountains in his homeland, beckoning him to ride their rhythms up and away through time.

It's the spring of 1893. He's nine years old and lying on the bed in his grandfather's cabin in the mountains of western North Carolina. Even though he is covered in a thick blanket, he is shivering from a three-day-old fever. Edward is sitting on the edge of the bed whittling a maple stick by the light of the moon, and their grandfather is again telling them the story of how he and their grandmother and hundreds of others refused to go on the Great March and vowed to never leave their homeland. John Francis has heard this story many times before, but there's something about his grandfather's searching eyes and rhythmic voice this time that's different, as if he is revealing something that has always been there but he's never seen. John Francis feels dizzy, so he shuts his eyes, and from behind closed lids watches in amazement as his grandfather's voice trots into his ear like a horse, her soft, white tail tickling his ear canal. She then canters down his throat to the middle of his chest, head high, eyes blazing, and prances in a circle, the vibrations radiating from his center outward. With one leap she bursts through his chest and John Francis grabs her white mane and swings his leg over her smooth back as they gallop upward, higher and higher above the cabin until they pierce the veil. Her hooves slide on the rocky mountain trail as they land and he sees his grandfather there, still a teenager, eyes staring at him out of a remote cave like a black fox. John Francis hears horses snort and whinny close by, and he looks down to see two soldiers with rifles slowly moving up the trail from below, heading right toward them. He turns back to the cave, his grandfather's eyes still on his, and nods once, the light passing between them. Then he takes off, the horse's mane flying around him as they jump off of the pass and into the dense forest below the soldiers, crashing loudly through the green. The soldiers jerk their horses around and race toward the hunt. John Francis crashes through the forest for another half mile, just out of their sight, then his horse leaps and they again take flight, racing higher and higher until they burst through the barrier. John Francis lands back in his grandfather's bed, his heart still galloping. He opens his eyes and Edward is gone, there is only silence, and his grandfather is sitting back in his chair, the moonlight streaming through the window, his eyes locked on John Francis's in gratitude.

Eleven years later John Francis steps out of a general store in a Mississippi town where he and Edward have been for a week working the harvest. He senses the wind before it blows, something he has finally become used to over the years, and looks around Edward and up the street to where the whispers are signaling him. She and her maid are walking toward them down the sidewalk, her watery green dress like a memory, her cheek turned down to the sleeping baby she holds in her arms. The back of her finger brushes the baby's face, and John Francis feels lifetimes roll through him like waves. His knees buckle and he grabs Edward's shoulder to steady himself. Edward elbows him hard in the side, whispers, "Boss's wife." The wind arrives and lifts her hair in wisps like a poem. John Francis forces his eyes down as Edward says something to her and he and Edward step off the sidewalk to let them pass. The weight of lifetimes bows his head as she walks by, and he knows with certainty that if he looks up and catches her eye, she will know. Edward shakes his head as John Francis watches her walk away from them down the sidewalk, the past and future swirling up and around her like dragonflies.

It's 1909, and he stands in an abandoned cotton

field, the dirt under his feet cracked like the back of an old man's hands. Dry husks of cotton plants surround him as far as he can see, eaten down to their stalks by boll weevils. Brown leaves blow across the porch of the abandoned white-columned house, and a broken window gapes like a missing tooth. It's been five years since he stood in this field. He has finally made his way back to her, so sure she would leave with him. The dried cotton plants rustle as the sun beats down on his neck and he sinks to his knees. In front of him the dirt splits and cracks open, huge fissures spreading across the landscape as a crow soars overhead, cawing mercilessly.

Time speeds up and flashes around him like lightning—his cousin's knuckles cracking his nose as whiskey-soaked words accuse him of thinking he is too good to live on the reservation. Two years later, Edward's shoulder touching his at the recruitment office. Scurrying through dark enemy fields ahead of the 36th Infantry, their Cherokee words gurgling through phone lines like river water over stones. The sun rising over lavender fields in Provence.

Time then collapses in upon itself. A brown spider dancing under crystal-clear water. A white swan gliding across a pale blue sky. Snow blowing off a roof and sparkling in the moonlight. A baby, his daughter, floating inside Rosemary like a new planet.

A blast reverberated through the night sky as Edward pulled John Francis's limp body onto his lap and cradled his head. John Francis was giddy, ecstatic, and he opened his mouth to tell Edward about his daughter, but the words poured out of the hole in his neck and soaked into Edward's pants. The night had gone strangely quiet, the sky was dark again, and for a moment the stars twinkled like a song. Then another blast, and machine-gun fire again whizzed through the air like comets.

Edward pulled him to his chest just as John Francis looked to the sky. There, galloping down from the moon, was their grandfather in his twenties on the white horse, red paint streaked in thick lines down both cheeks. He caught John Francis's eyes in his and nodded, then landed a few yards behind Edward's back. The horse reared and kicked her front feet as his grandfather held her mane with one hand, then they galloped away from John Francis and Edward, stomping and whooping into the night. The last thing John Francis heard was confused German voices barking as they moved toward the commotion and away from them.

John Francis's eyes closed as the world slipped into silence. Then he heard whinnying, first far away, then getting closer and closer. A gust of wind picked him up, and he circled like a leaf over Edward, alone at the edge of the clearing, holding his body and sobbing. He heard the whinnying again, this time much closer, and he looked to his left to see his grandfather riding the galloping horse toward him in the sky.

His grandfather held his hand out to him as he passed, and John Francis grabbed it and pulled himself up onto her back. They raced higher and higher and then through the barrier, his homeland now below them, fog rolling down the green mountainsides like seafoam. They grazed the treetops, then his grandfather slid off the horse, his feet touching the earth. John Francis watched as his grandfather stroked the horse's neck and then lowered his head, pressing his forehead to hers. Immediately John Francis absorbed into the horse's skin like mist. He neighed and shook his mane as his grandfather let go and stepped back, and once again the light passed between them.

Then John Francis leapt into the sky, his hooves

bounding over clouds as he raced northbound, higher and higher, lighter and lighter, toward home.

nine

"He [The Great Spirit] only sketches out the path of life roughly for all the creatures on earth, shows them where to go, where to arrive, but leaves them to find their own way to get there. He wants them to act independently according to their nature, to the urges of each of them."

—Lame Deer

December 26, 1934

Murphy, North Carolina

"Hey, Chief, don't forget your bag."

Fifty-two-year-old Edward swiveled his head around from the rushing landscape as the freight train slowed, the whiskey sloshing behind his eyes. Leroy held out a small, tattered duffle bag and Edward took it, smiled at his old friend, and turned back to the open door of the boxcar. The whole world was white, the full moon shining off of the freshly fallen snow.

Edward was going to miss Leroy. He was from south Alabama and had been riding the rails with him the past ten years, sometimes working the harvest, sometimes panhandling, sometimes finding a warm woman and sharing her bed for the night. Leroy was a good man, probably the best friend Edward had ever had besides his brother. Edward felt the familiar pain surge through him. Sixteen years later, no matter how much whiskey he drank, just the thought of John Francis broke through the numbness like a toothache.

The train was at the sweet spot, slowed down enough for him to jump as far from the deadly screeching wheels as possible, but not so slow that the bulls, the railroad's hired thugs, would be close enough to catch him. Edward jumped, his worn knees buckling as his feet hit the embankment, his bag flying out of his hand as he crumpled and rolled head over feet through the snow. It took a moment, but he was able to stand up and brush off his pants. As he picked his bag out of a briar patch, he looked up to see the outline of Leroy waving to him from the boxcar before disappearing back into the darkness.

Edward made his way to the road and began walking toward Grape Creek, past rotten walls and caved-in roofs. The snow softened the jagged edges and hollow sounds, and the moon up ahead beckoned him like a light. After several miles, his eighty-year-old mother's house waited up ahead on the right. After Edward's mother got married to his father, the State of North Carolina finally recognized some of the wrongs they had committed against the Cherokee people, and though his grandfather had to pay for what was rightfully his in the first place, he was able to keep the land he had been squatting on for decades. Edward and John Francis's father had built their mother a house down the mountain from their grandfather's cabin. Edward could make out the outline of the stone chimney he and John Francis had built for her the summer before they left for the first time. Thirty-two years later it was still standing.

Grey smoke poured from the chimney and light flickered in the living room, and he knew that she was sitting in her rocking chair reading. By the end of the week, she would get the letter he mailed the day before. Edward pulled the flask out of his pocket and took a long drink.

When they were boys and their father was still alive, they would gather in the living room after supper and their mother, who cleaned houses during the day, would read them stories, sometimes in Cherokee, other times in English. When they were old enough to read themselves, they would take turns reading to her. On Edward's favorite nights, he and John Francis would walk the winding horse trail up the mountain behind her house to their grandfather's cabin for stories. Their grandfather never learned to speak English, but the stories he told in Cherokee would come alive in front of Edward's eyes in a way the written ones couldn't.

Edward turned and found the overgrown trail behind her house leading up the mountain. He didn't look back as he made his ascent.

When their grandfather died in 1909, he and John Francis buried him at the base of the maple behind his cabin. The next morning John Francis told Edward he had a vision that he and the woman he loved, Rosemary, were merged into one, half her, half him. To John Francis, that meant he was supposed to go get her and bring her back to live with him at the cabin. Never mind that she was married with six children, or that her husband had a bounty on their heads, or that she was used to an easy life, not a mountain cabin life. Edward had tried to talk him out of going back to Mississippi to get her, but John Francis would not listen. He said this was his destiny, he was sure of it. The stars had told him.

Two weeks later, when he came back without her, it was as if he had stepped off the trail and was lost in the forest, walking in circles.

Years later, after John Francis's body was buried in a French battlefield, Edward knocked three times on an alleyway door and he and Leroy slinked into a speakeasy in downtown Memphis. The air immediately fell an octave. He looked to his right to see Rosemary's husband William laughing with a prostitute no older than eighteen on his lap, his wedding ring glinting from around her waist. Edward nudged Leroy and without a word they ducked back out the unmarked door.

The old trail kept winding up and up, and Edward had to stop twice, his breath rasping in white bursts. He had been homeless so long he didn't know what home felt like anymore. He tried to feel the earth under his feet, the wind on his cheek, the bare branches as he brushed past them. But all he felt was alone.

The trail finally opened up to a clearing, and in the middle stood his grandfather's hundred-year-old cabin. The roof sagged and the front door was missing, but the log walls stood strong. Edward felt a sense of home wash over him for a fleeting moment, then it was gone again.

The snow was silent under his boots as he walked past the cabin and toward the old maple behind it. The wind blew a spray of snow from the roof as he passed, snowflakes glittering around him in the moonlight. When he got to the maple he stopped, sat down at the base where her trunk merged with the earth, and set his bag on the snow beside him. He leaned back against the cold bark and closed his eyes.

The week before, Edward had had his own vision while kneeling beside Leroy as blood pumped out of the knife wound in his friend's heart. He was no longer in the filthy Hooverville in Virginia with the white men running away from them in the dark, but sitting at the base of the maple, like he was now, new life beginning to sprout in green shoots all around him. John Francis, maybe ten years old, came running up to him, and turned into a bear cub right in front of Edward's eyes. He then scrambled up the tree, his sharp claws scratching the bark as he scampered higher and higher. The earth had opened up next to Edward, and he looked down to see thousands of bones. He instantly knew they were his ancestors', his grandmother and grandfather's, his and John Francis's.

The shrill of a police siren jerked him back to Leroy gurgling, but in the darkness all he heard was John Francis's voice saying, "Home, home," in Cherokee over and over until all of Leroy's blood had soaked into the dirt.

Leroy's spirit had stayed by his side as Edward made his way back home, their final trip together.

Edward opened his eyes hoping to see John Francis there, but only the snow winked back at him. He reached into his bag and pulled out John Francis's penny-sized dog tags. They clinked as Edward slipped the chain over his head and slid them under his shirt, the metal discs cold against his chest. Edward may not have been able to save his brother, but at least he had made it home with the only thing he had left of him.

That consolation was fragile, a thin layer of ice.

Edward reached back into his bag and pulled out the towel-wrapped poison hemlock roots. When he left Virginia the dark-eyed gypsy had told him that one of what she called "devil's bread" would be more than enough, but he had pulled three of the wild-parsnip-looking roots from the drainage ditch where she told him just in case.

They were bitter and musty, but he managed to eat

all three of them. He then slipped his brother's dog tags over his neck, slid them off of the chain, and swallowed them, too, the metal scratching his throat all the way down.

Edward leaned back on the trunk. It was just a matter of time now. All he wanted was to feel connected one last time to his home like he had when he and John Francis ran barefoot all through these woods. He felt a cloud rolling down from the mountain toward him, like the morning fog he used to love as a boy. He felt excitement stir inside him. Back then, no matter where he was, he always knew which way to go. But as the cloud inched closer, he saw that this time it was dark, violent, swirling with regrets and failures.

And he realized he was a fool to think that he could find his way back home after all this time.

In an instant sixteen years of sedation evaporated and he was vulnerably sober. Then the world around him started whirling, spinning, and swaying. His heart started racing as he felt the blackness rolling closer and closer, picking up steam like a freight train bearing down on him. The urge to run overtook him and he tried to stand, but he couldn't feel or move anything from his waist down. And the paralysis was creeping up his body.

Somewhere in front of him something moved, so he squeezed his eyes shut and then opened them again. There, in front of him like in his vision, was ten-year-old John Francis running toward him. He wasn't alone after all. John Francis had come to save him.

Edward looked up the mountain to see that the blackness was just at the edge of the tree line and racing toward them. John Francis transformed into the bear cub and then leapt over Edward's head, his paws hugging the maple's trunk. His claws scratched and scraped as he scrambled up higher and higher, the blackness just a few feet from the base of the tree. Edward watched helplessly as John Francis scurried up and out of his sight, and it finally occurred to him that John Francis had not come to save him. He may have come to show him the way, but the only person who could save him was himself. Edward felt the shackles of paralysis break open and he bounded up the tree, following his brother.

Edward was blinded by the darkness and the acrid black filled his nose, mouth, and ears with soot as it overtook him, but he kept climbing. He knew his brother was up high, higher than the blackness, higher than the failures and regrets, higher than the guilt. Edward coughed and burned and spit and gagged, but he kept going. And then, like in the eye of a great storm, he poked his head up to the clear, moonlit sky. John Francis was gone, absorbed into the stars, yet Edward had never felt less alone in his whole life.

As he climbed the rest of the way to the top of the tree, the darkness rolled by and kept going, and he could suddenly see his grandfather's cabin, his mother's house, his homeland for miles. He looked down and saw that he was naked and that his skin was glowing, as if he was lit from the inside out. It was as if he had shed his skin, translucent shells of his former self left behind. And he knew he had finally made it.

Something up the mountain rustled, the moon began to sing, and he could hear the bones beneath him calling him home. Green shoots began popping up through the snow as the earth below him opened up and held her arms out to catch him.

So he took a deep breath, closed his eyes, and jumped.

ten

"When we become hollow bones there is no limit to what the Higher Powers can do in and through us in spiritual things."

—Frank Fools Crow

February 27, 1973

Sugar Tree, Tennessee

Margaret unlocked the front door at the top of the stairs of the Treehouse, a one-room stilt house just up the road from the Tennessee River where she and Carl had moved after he retired and they sold their downtown Memphis high-rise apartment in 1970. The emptiness waited in the dim room like an old friend as Margaret stepped inside and flipped on the light. She set the plastic box and her purse down on the yellow Formica table and then pulled back the thick brown curtains from the sliding glass door. Shelves of books stared back at her from the paneled walls, a cobweb floated on the bottom corner of the shelf above the sink, and the brown plant in the pot on the windowsill beside the bed curled in on itself like a dead spider. Margaret turned back to the door and shut it.

It had been three weeks since she had found Carl at the bottom of the stairs. She had sat on the dirt beside his body for over an hour until Tom, the biker down the road, gently lifted her by the arm and led her back up the stairs. She stayed with her daughter Carla, her husband, and their two young children in Pine Bluff, Arkansas, for the cremation and funeral, but then, ignoring Carla's demands to stay, Margaret drove Carl's 1965 Camaro the six hours back to Sugar Tree with Carl in the nondescript black plastic box on the seat beside her, the sun in her rearview mirror.

Margaret sat down at the table and stared at Carl's remains. Forty-six years of marriage reduced to a six-by-four-inch temporary urn.

Memphis, 1927, just a few months before the rain-swollen Mississippi River poured over the levees and spread for miles, she was standing outside the dance when he had pulled up in a light blue Model T. Whispers about bootlegging excited her, and she knew by the way he looked at her all she had to do was part her lips just enough for the streetlight to catch the glimmer. He was from Corinth, Mississippi, and even though she had lived in Memphis since she was three years old, she was originally from Abbeville, Mississippi. He had dropped out of high school to support his mother, she had quit, bored, after the tenth grade. By the end of the first date they were steaming up the windows in the back seat of the Model T. By the end of the first month they were married.

Margaret touched the box, the plastic unnaturally smooth. Once, when she was nine years old, Margaret squeezed out the window at the sweltering tenement house in downtown Memphis and skipped behind her older brothers to the public pool down the street. She knew she would get punished when she got back home; ever since she could remember, her mother, Miss Rosemary as the old man next door called her, had forbidden her to go near the water. It seemed her mother was afraid of everything, rarely leaving their house, jumping from cracks of lightning, keeping her eyes down as she placed the boiled potatoes on the table. But the pool was calling to Margaret like a song, and to feel its cool softness against her skin was worth the solitary confinement later. Her swimming cap had felt strangely smooth, like an egg over her dark hair.

It had been Margaret's idea for Carl to buy the Treehouse and move out of the city. She just couldn't stand one more year of people crammed on top of each other, loud cars, concrete sidewalks. Despite people everywhere, she spent almost all of her time alone, even with Carl sitting beside her. Their weekend trips to the Holly Springs National Forest just weren't enough anymore. All she had to say was that she wanted to live in the middle of trees near the water, and Carl turned in his retirement notice at the elevator company and put their apartment on the market. It was the flowing river water that fascinated her, not the still water in lakes, and when she read about how the Tennessee River was formed from the French Broad River, the third oldest river in the world and even older than the North Carolina mountains it flowed out of, she knew where to tell Carl to look.

Margaret stood back up just as the phone on the wall rang. "Oh, for the love of Pete," she said aloud. She knew it was Marvin. She knew he had been watching the road the past couple of weeks, waiting for her to drive up. She also knew that he had feigned being Carl's friend since they moved in. The real reason he showed up uninvited was to see her. Here she was, sixty-nine years old, and eyes still watched her no matter where she went.

Men had hovered around her her entire life. Once, when she was thirteen, Johnny Baker pushed her back against a tree and tried to kiss her. She kneed him hard in the crotch and then walked away, head held high, as his friends laughed. When he befriended her older brother Samuel the next year, she made it a point to slip out the back door every time he came over.

Women, on the other hand, eyed her like whispers. From the time she was a teenager, Margaret could walk into a room and a pathway would clear as heads turned her way and women leaned in closer to their men. Margaret could see their thoughts and intentions as clear as she saw their staring eyes. She knew more about people than they knew about themselves, just as she knew which was the green spool of thread with her eyes closed, just as she knew her father was in the young landlady's bed on Saturday nights. She also knew that her mother, who was like a candle that had been blown out before Margaret was born, carried long-held secrets deep inside.

Margaret had learned to work with the knowing, even use it to her advantage when she needed to, but it had its price. The only person she had ever let in even a crack was Carl. She'd even kept their only child at arm's length, not because she didn't want to love Carla, but because she didn't know how to.

She did love Carl, inasmuch as she was able to. In return he was her shield, deflecting stares, jealousies, and insecurities like a mirror. It had never occurred to her that he would one day leave her alone and unprotected.

Margaret crossed her arms in front of her as the phone rang again. She then picked up Carl's ashes, turned her back to the sound, and opened the sliding glass door to the deck.

Margaret slid the door shut behind her and unsealed the top of the plastic urn. Carl floated effortlessly to the ground, spreading over and among the fallen leaves.

∞ ∞ ∞

Margaret's skin tingled and prickled as if currents of electricity were pulsating through her. She opened her eyes and glanced at the clock on her nightstand, the red numbers glowing in the dark. 5:55 a.m. She blinked. :55 a.m. And that's when she knew the migraine was starting. It was as if a void opened up in her field of vision that she was helpless to close. No matter how hard she tried to stop them, the flickering lights came next, like shards of blinding red, green, blue, and white glass first shattering out of the void and then taking over everything, slicing and cutting her ties to her own sanity, their intensity ripping the two-dimensional reality of everyday life. She knew what was coming next but was unable to stop it. In a matter of minutes the shards began to join ends and create a pulsating circle, a portal of sorts, that then spewed nightmarish half-formed images in deafening colors and scalding gyrations. Her head pounded mercilessly, bile crawled up her throat like acid, and flames raced across her skin like a wildfire. She was completely helpless, trapped in the pain like a prisoner. And Carl was scattered in the woods. It could last two hours or twelve, she had no way to control it. She felt like it was hunting her, stalking her through a thick jungle as she ran blindly. All she knew to do was to keep running. She would not go down without a fight.

∞ ∞ ∞

It was late afternoon before the migraine had subsided enough for Margaret to get out of bed. Her legs were unsteady as she walked to the bathroom, splashed water on her face, and brushed her teeth. The well water tasted tinny, metallic, as it ran down her throat. Her bloodshot eyes were like forests of tiny red trees.

She changed into blue jeans and tied a light blue scarf around her salt-and-pepper hair. She would have to wash it in the morning. She needed to get to the Sugar Tree Market before Velma closed at 5 p.m.

The first thing she saw when she closed her front door was Marvin's yellow note pinned to it with a red thumbtack. He saw she was back, was worried about her, and would stop by again after supper to check on her. Margaret ripped the note off, the thumbtack bouncing down the stairs and into the dead leaves.

Velma grumbled when Margaret opened the front door of the market, but she let her get coffee, a can of tuna, a loaf of sliced bread. Margaret sat in the small gravel parking lot, engine running, as Velma locked up and drove off.

The sky was beginning to fade. Margaret stared blankly out of her windshield at the aqua green cinderblock building. The last thing she wanted was to have to deal with Marvin, but she couldn't just sit here all night. Then, in the silence, she thought she heard the faint sound of singing. It was watery, strange, and not like anything she had ever heard before. For some reason it made her think of the river down the road, and then *Bewitched,* their teak Chris-Craft Constellation, docked at the Cherokee Boat Dock two miles away. It was a gift from Carl the day they closed on the Treehouse. Her favorite memories since moving here were driving the boat on sunset cruises or waking up on the water and watching the sun rise over the sleepy river. But she had never been out there without Carl.

Margaret backed up, turned around, and passed the turnoff to her road as she headed toward the boat dock.

She parked the car in their usual spot, grabbed her bag of groceries, and walked down the covered dock. *Bewitched* sat in their slip, her sleek, curved sides reflecting the shadow of the water. It was quiet as Margaret boarded, just the lapping of the water against the dock, the other boats gently rocking. She stepped down into the cabin, put the groceries on the galley's counter, and slid open the door to the queen-sized stateroom. Like everything else since Carl's death, it looked bigger, full of empty space. She turned and walked back up top and pulled the key out of the unlocked cubby under the steering wheel. The red and white foam keychain bobbed like a buoy as she put it in the ignition.

The sun was starting to make its last statement of the day in pinks and purples as Margaret untied the ropes just like she had seen Carl do, sat down in the captain's chair, and turned on the engine. It sputtered at first and then rolled to life, and she carefully backed out of the slip. She slowly made her way out of the no-wake zone and onto the main channel of the Tennessee River.

A cardinal was the first one to get her attention, his red wings darting through the pines alongside the shoreline. Then a bigger blueish-black bird, a crow, glided over the water in front of the bow. Margaret pulled the throttle down halfway and picked up speed, the late February wind cool on her face, as a blue heron, neck curved back in an S, flapped up from the sandy bank and flew several yards with her before setting back down. Then an eagle, wingspan wider than she was tall, soared overhead, circled once, and floated toward the tree line.

Margaret felt lightheaded, that strange sensation of being on the cusp between day and night, as she veered toward her favorite wooded cove.

She slowed down and glided into the undeveloped cove, then cut the engine as she turned the boat back to face the entrance. Her own wake rocked the boat gently side to side, the lapping of the water against the wooden hull the only sound. After a moment she walked to the stern, dropped the anchor until it dug in and set itself, and then pulled out a lounge chair and opened it on the deck. The sun set completely, leaving only darkness in its wake.

Margaret settled into the chair and looked up to the grey-black sky, her eyes searching for the round face of the moon. The stars glistened like young girls. Margaret shivered, though not from cold, and she realized that without Carl there, it was if she had taken off a light layer, a thin shawl. She didn't know how long she would be there or even what she was doing on the boat at all. All she knew was that she was exactly where she was supposed to be.

In the distance Margaret heard the watery singing

again, so faint it could have just been the breeze. There was something so familiar about it, yet something she knew she had never heard until that day. As she watched the night sky the watery singing became louder and clearer, women's voices and words she'd never heard but somehow knew. They rocked her like a lullaby and for the first time in many years she allowed herself to feel vulnerable, childlike. Her eyes followed a shooting star across the sky, a trail of stardust sparkling behind it.

The absence started in the corner of her left eye, as if the stars that were there were suddenly sucked into a void and only darkness was left. Margaret's hands clenched the armrests as the familiar panic began to rise like heatwaves and a shard of white flickering light shattered out of the void and hurled toward her. But then the watery singing poured in through her eyes, ears, and nose in pastel colors, washing away the jagged shard of flickering light and replacing it with the universe in a drop of water.

The watery singing filled the void, and though she didn't understand the language, Margaret knew what the voices were telling her.

Let go.

She felt herself expand as she took a long, slow breath. What remained of the world around her fell away as she dove deep into the void and then resurfaced where the French Broad River was born at the junction of North Fork and West Fork in North Carolina. She watched as her clothes, skin, and bones dissolved and she became the ancient water itself, flowing with currents, allowing the whole to take her along with it as she curved through mountains she'd visited somewhere in her dreams, flowing northwest and picking up pieces of herself along the way as she meandered through western North Carolina then Tennessee, merging with the Holston River to become the Tennessee River and then coursing southwest to Alabama before turning northward through central Tennessee and past Sugar Tree, the singing no longer outside but now inside her, the boat rocking beneath her as she flowed under it and continued north to the mouth of the Ohio River and then westward to merge with the Mississippi, her currents swirling with the currents of all of the tributaries as they turned south, merging into one, flowing along the border of Mississippi and Arkansas and then through Louisiana toward the Gulf of Mexico.

And as Margaret emptied into the ocean in a song

that connected to all the other oceans, she flowed under a small boat carrying a green-eyed child, her granddaughter, bobbing on the waves, her hand dangling off the side, her fingertips skimming the surface as concentric circles rippled outward.

eleven

"My friends, how desperately do we need to be loved and to love."

—Chief Dan George

September 30, 2003

Little Rock, Arkansas

Carla laid her head back on the hard hospital bed and gazed out the window. Her once-sun-filled auburn hair was just grey tufts now, sticking out randomly, brittle to the touch. It was morning, sometime before noon, and the sky was robin's-egg blue like the scarf her mother Margaret wore every day the month before she died. That was twenty-four years ago in this same hospital, St. Vincent Infirmary, two floors up, Room 602. Carla's eyelids were heavy as she slowly turned her head away from the window. The taupe chair was empty; her daughter Anna must have gone outside again to smoke. Her hand, purple-splotched and thin like a baby bird, lay on top of her tattered Bible on the bed beside her. The medicine dripping down the clear plastic tube into her arm was heavy, a thick blanket blocking out the pain. Last month the oncologist had sat her and Anna down and told them that the egg-sized tumor at the base of her skull was inoperable.

If only the medicine could smother the never-ending reel playing in her mind.

Frank, the cheerful nurse who had told her he was thirty-three, the same age as her son Jacob, appeared out of the haze and began poking and prodding. Carla remembered how her mother had snapped at every nurse each time they came into her room in the hospital in Jackson, Tennessee, after she had fallen and broken her hip, and how she had demanded Carla take her back home to Sugar Tree when she was released. Carla lied and told her she would. Her mother had no business being up there alone at her age. After Carla's father had died six years before, her mother had become a recluse, refusing to leave Sugar Tree or even answer the phone half the time. The only real contact she had was with her neighbor, Marvin, but that was only once a week when he brought her groceries and cigarettes, and he told Carla he had to hand the bags to her through the door. Carla was tired of worrying about her mother and the stress of it all. She had had enough on her plate after the divorce. The five-hour drive from Jackson to Carla's home in Little Rock had been silent, her mother glaring out the window the whole time. Two months later she had died upstairs alone in a cold hospital bed.

Frank was asking Carla how she was feeling, if there was anything she needed, what number the pain was from one to ten. Carla remembered being ten years old and riding the Ferris Wheel at the Memphis Zoo, wedged between her mother and father as the big wheel turned. Her father had stroked her mother's hair over Carla's head and then leaned over and kissed her for a full rotation as if Carla wasn't there. In some ways, she supposed she never really was. The lion cage had looked strange from up high, a bird's-eye view of a big cat trapped behind thick steel bars. That night Carla had woken up with the hot dog, cotton candy, and soda spewing out of her mouth and nose all over her pink eyelet comforter and hardwood floor. Her father had flipped on the light and then slipped in the puddle. She could hear her mother grumbling behind the master bedroom door as her father led her to the bathtub. Later that night she heard her mother asking her father why they couldn't go back to the cabin in the Holly Springs National Forest, just the two of them, and stay there forever.

Frank was gone now, the room once again full of empty silence. Carla had never been comfortable in silence. It needed to be filled up with sounds, syllables, words. Without them the thoughts crept back in like the shadows of thieves.

St. Joseph Hospital in Memphis, 1957. She was sixteen years old. The excruciating cramping had started less than an hour earlier, followed by bright red blood and meaty clots. Carlos, Johnny's best friend, had carried her into the emergency room as Johnny, who was Black, nervously waited in the car in the parking lot of the Whites-Only hospital. For years her father had ranted nonstop about how the Goldsteins shouldn't be allowed to join the Chickasaw Country Club. She knew better than to tell him she was in love with Johnny. She was too scared to tell anyone about missing her period for three months, so she pretended it wasn't happening. Until the cramping started. The short, stocky nun had come into her room with thin lips and a silent stare after the blue-veined baby, no bigger than an avocado and encased in his own rubbery bubble, had plopped into the cold, metal bowl. Without a word, the nun had walked out with the bowl, the door shutting behind her. A priest had prayed over Carlos in the waiting room while Carla slept. The next morning she walked out of the hospital wearing her blood-stained dress.

Carla told no one. She pledged Chi Omega at the University of Arkansas, married a Pine Bluff, Arkansas, banker in 1964, put on red lipstick for her husband's office parties and dinners. She learned how to nod and smile at the right time, especially when the wives would start talking about the audacity of the Negroes, especially that one troublemaker, Martin Luther King, Jr. Carla only saw her parents a few times a year, always when she drove to Memphis, as her mother would not come to Pine Bluff to visit.

It wasn't until 1967 in her third trimester with Anna that she had the first nightmare. Fluids steaming as her baby's curled-up body, semitransparent like a skinned plum, was hurled into an incinerator. Metal bowl crumpling and tiny bones snapping as they were crushed in a trash compactor. Water splashing as the toilet flushed and carried her baby deep into the bowels of St. Joseph's. Carla, blood pouring down her legs, running through the slick white hospital halls, desperately searching.

After that the nightmares would come and go, jolting her awake. The condo in Destin. The morning after Jacob's birth. The first night in their new house in Little Rock. Shame and guilt would swell up like a blister and she would lash out at whomever was closest: her husband, the checkout lady at Kroger, the children.

After the divorce and her mother's death, Carla found an unexpected kinship and was baptized into the Catholic church. Father Malone repeatedly reminded her that confession absolved her of her sins, but her past was like a scab that she kept picking at, never allowing the wound to heal. Her biggest failures were Anna and Jacob. Both were unable to find their way. Anna was defiant, strong-headed, taking any chance she got to argue about the hypocrisies of organized religion, especially Catholicism. Jacob was sensitive, dependent, unable to break the grip of addiction that had stripped away his dignity and self-respect. The thought of leaving them behind made her heart split open, the pain breaking through the narcotics. Because they had not been saved, they would end up suffering for eternity, just like her mother and first baby. She had failed at leading them to salvation. With her gone, they wouldn't know how to find their way.

Out of the corner of her eye Carla thought she saw movement, so she turned her heavy head toward the window. There, perched on the windowsill four stories high, was a robin. Its head was cocked sideways, and for a moment Carla could swear that its black eye was looking directly at her. She vaguely remembered a story about how a brave robin flew up to Jesus on the cross and tried to pluck the crown of thorns away with his beak, but it tore the robin's breast instead. Carla closed her eyes and felt the familiar pain as sharp thorns ripped into the tender flesh of her chest and lodged there, once again paying penance for the sins she had committed, staining her chest with bright red blood for all the world to see. It was relieving, almost ecstatic, if only for a fleeting moment.

The emptiness in the room started pressing down on her. Carla opened her eyes to see that the robin was gone, just the sky left in its place. She felt a darkness, as if a cold front was making its way up from her feet to her head. Twenty-four years ago Carla had gone home to take a shower, the first time she had left her mother's side in thirty-six hours. When she got back, the nurse stopped her at the station and told her that her mother was gone. Carla's knees had buckled. Her mother had died alone. As Carla looked at the empty chair, she realized the pattern was about to repeat itself.

Carla was paralyzed with fear when she felt someone watching her. She turned her head to see a shadowy figure standing next to her bed, reaching a hand toward her hand on the Bible. Relief coursed through her. Anna had made it in time. But then her vision cleared and she saw that it wasn't Anna after all. It was her mother, blue scarf and hospital gown, as if she had just walked down from Room 602. And she grasped Carla's hand.

The room began spinning as she felt herself lifting up from her body on the bed. She squeezed her eyes shut as the wind rotated around them. When she opened them she and her mother were in a large grassy field next to a flowing river, their bare feet touching down on the earth. Carla could see the top of St. Joseph's a few blocks away. Her mother placed Carla's hand on a maple tree, its bark wet with sap.

Suddenly Carla felt the ground trembling. The sap absorbed into her skin and flowed down to her feet, and she felt her roots sprout and bury deep into the soil. The roots became eyes and she saw hundreds and hundreds of little bones lined up in rows, unborn babies in unmarked graves, their pine boxes absorbed back into the soil. The tip of her root curled through a tiny skull, and she knew at once that it was her and Johnny's baby, found at last, buried like a lost treasure in the earth. He had been here all along.

Carla was once again standing on top of the earth, her hand still pressed against the maple. She looked around to see that her mother was gone. But she was no longer afraid of being alone. She reached down and pulled the thorns out of her chest and dropped them. She felt the tumor in the back of her head crack open, and a tiny white bird flew out and landed in front of her on the grass. It grew bigger and bigger until it was a swan, her long neck curved and graceful.

The sky above her opened up, and Carla watched as the Blessed Virgin Mary appeared in the clouds and held her arms open wide. Carla climbed on the back of the swan, her feathers soft and downy, her neck thin yet firm in Carla's hands. They flew up and up and up, the swan's great wings lifted by the air, Carla's hair once again auburn and filled with sunlight.

"… everything on the earth has a purpose, every
disease an herb to cure it, and every person a mission.
This is the Indian theory of existence."

—Mourning Dove Salish

February 22, 2017

Little Rock, Arkansas

Jacob's hip ached as he hobbled three cars down and plucked the five-dollar bill from the cracked window of the white SUV and the light turned green. His body creaked and groaned like it was eighty-seven, not forty-seven. The grass median on Highway 10 at the I-430 exit ramp was brown and dry; *Anything Helps* begged from his cardboard sign. The cars all looked the same—blurs of eyes looking straight ahead when the light was green, down or sideways when it was red. He had gotten to where he could tell a giver several cars away. It was a good-enough exchange, a symbiotic relationship. This five made eighty-seven dollars for the day. That was going to have to do. The pain of living was breaking through and he needed another fix.

He coughed as he made his way to his untagged car in the parking lot of the sprawling white church two blocks away. The last time he had been in a church was for his mother Carla's funeral at Good Council Catholic Church fourteen years earlier. He had stood in the back the whole time. He wasn't allowed to take communion anyway, and besides, he was too high to talk to anyone. He knew his sister Anna had seen him before he slipped out. She always did.

Jacob pushed the crumpled fast-food bags over and sat heavily on the dirt-crusted seat. His teacup Chihuahua Sweet Pea jumped on his lap and he scooped her up in one hand and let her lick his beard. He had gotten her last year as a birthday present for his second wife Tracey, but Tracey was gone again, disappeared to who knows where for over a week now. Sweet Pea was really his dog, anyway. He pulled out a day-old fry and fed it to her, her tail wagging giddily.

The phone buzzed in his back pocket. Rachel would meet him within the hour at his tattered pop-up camper, which was parked down a dirt road behind a barn on the side of a pond. He'd been squatting on a friend of a friend's twenty acres outside the city limits for three months now. No neighbors, no cops, no hassles. No one knew where he was unless he wanted them to. Two weeks ago he ran out of gas for the generator, but decided he didn't need lights or constant sound, anyway. Flashlights and candles were doing just fine. He hoped Rachel brought needles this time. He was in no shape to have to go get some. He started the car, lit a joint with trembling hands, and pulled out of the parking lot.

∞ ∞ ∞

A shiny electric car sat at the end of his dirt road, turned around, backed up to the barn. He knew it was her before he saw her. How in the world she knew how to find him he didn't know. But it really didn't surprise him. She had been that way since they were kids.

Jacob hadn't seen or talked to his older sister Anna in five years. That wasn't necessarily a bad thing. Unlike just about everyone else, including their dad, Jacob hadn't burned a bridge with Anna, mainly because they hadn't asked anything from each other. As kids she would pick him to be on her kickball team, play ping-pong on the back porch for hours, say hi to him in the school halls. She moved away and he stayed behind, sliding deeper and deeper into addiction. When she moved back, got married, and had kids, Jacob occasionally showed up on holidays. Four years ago, when he heard that her husband had left her and her two young children for a twenty-two-year-old waitress, he had dialed her number several times, but then never hit send. Sometimes, nothing is the best thing someone can offer.

He pulled himself out of the car and limped toward her as she got out of hers. People always locked down around him, as if his addiction was contagious, or he was going to take from them something they didn't want to give. Even Anna. He didn't blame them, really. He wouldn't trust him, either. But as he awkwardly hugged her, he noticed Anna was unnervingly relaxed, her smile genuine. He hadn't seen her like this since they were kids.

She hadn't come to check on him, she said, or ask anything from him. She had just woken up that day, gone for a run, and found an owl feather on the trail.

Something told her she needed to find him, give it to him, and show him that she was okay. She had made it through the divorce, she and the kids were happy. And for reasons she didn't understand, she needed him to know that.

Jacob felt her words swirling around his brain. Anna was a writer and had always been dreamy, airy, like the wind that picked up dead leaves and spun them. She would talk about plants and animals, rocks and trees like they were teachers, as if that was what normal people talked about at dinner. He always had the feeling she knew more than she was letting on, and he watched many times as people gravitated away from her. It was like she knew things about them they didn't even know about themselves, or want to know. He had never been able to connect in the way he felt she wanted to. He wondered if anyone ever really had. But something about what she was saying resonated, striking a place deep in him that he couldn't quite reach. And he let it reverberate through him as he took the feather.

Five minutes later Anna was pointing at the sky through the driver's window as she drove away. A Great Horned Owl floated silently overhead, the late afternoon sun reflecting off of his tan-and-white wings.

Jacob watched as Anna passed Rachel driving toward him on the other side of the road, dust curling up behind her car like smoke.

∞ ∞ ∞

The heroin tingled up his arm and then exploded, warmth spreading through his body in waves of bliss. Jacob laid his head back and closed his eyes as the needle fell on the bare mattress. As soon as he opened his eyes each morning, he felt like a thick rope was tied to his ankle, binding him to the world, a slave bound to his master. Being high was the only time he even remotely felt slack in the line. He was vaguely aware of Rachel beside him talking about how her old man had just gotten out of the pen.

The sun setting through the small window…

… Sweet Pea burying her nose in his neck …

∞ ∞ ∞

The eerie yipping and howling of the coyotes started off far away, reaching like a hand through the bliss. Jacob slowly opened his heavy eyes and tried to focus.

It was pitch-black, the only light the white of the moon outside the open camper door. The room buzzed like radio static. He could hear Rachel breathing heavily beside him. The rise and fall of the howling faded around him as he closed his eyes again, allowing the euphoria to cover him once again like a blanket.

∞ ∞ ∞

Jacob's head pounded as he forced his eyes open. Daybreak had come quietly like a thief, stealing the bliss and leaving a cold emptiness in its place. He pushed himself up on one elbow, scratched his beard, cleared his throat. Rachel was gone. Something wasn't right, but he couldn't quite put his finger on it. His legs ached as he stood up, lit a cigarette, and then stepped outside.

He didn't really notice the frogs at first. They were more of a low humming noise, like one of those nature CDs people listen to to relax. He relieved himself in a briar thicket, walked to the pond, and dipped his hands in the cool water. The frogs started croaking louder, and then louder, filling Jacob's ears and coursing through his body like water. He looked up to see rainclouds moving in quickly, dirty grey filling up the sky. Thunder rumbled in the distance, a strike of lightning shot from a rain-swollen cloud. And then, just like that, the frogs all became silent. Jacob stood up slowly.

The open camper door. Coyotes yipping and howling. Sweet Pea.

The first raindrop splattered on his head as he took two big strides and called her name loud and sharp. He had to get around the pond to the woods on the other side. He stumbled over rocks and roots as the sky opened and the rain shot down in fat drops. Halfway around he yelled her name again, this time louder, sharper. The only sound he could hear was the blood pumping through his veins. No barking, no howling, no croaking.

Rachel's scream splintered the sky behind him. Jacob turned to see her stumbling forward in the rain, a bald guy pushing her from behind as they came from the barn toward the pond. Rachel fell on her knees and the guy kicked her in the back and kept stomping toward Jacob. Rachel screamed again, this time Jacob's name, but he turned back around. He was almost to the woods to find Sweet Pea.

The gunshot broke the air over the pond like glass, shattering it into a million pieces. Jacob felt the bullet pierce his back and streak through his chest like a shooting star, leaving a trail of stardust in its wake. He fell face-forward, the damp moss soft under his right cheek. He closed his eyes as his hearing zoomed in like a laser: another scream, yelling, an engine revving, tires pressing into mud. Then silence.

The rain pelted his back as his blood ran out and soaked into the moss. There was no pain, no emptiness. It was glorious, the high he'd been chasing his entire life, the ecstasy of floating and not being tethered to the earth. If only he could stay here forever.

The clinking of metal tinkled around him, and Jacob used the last of his strength to open his left eye. Sweet Pea was in front of him, her tail wagging giddily, nuzzling her nose into his cheek. And that's when he knew.

She was okay. She had made it out alive. Just like Anna.

Jacob felt himself unfurl from his body. The rain slowed to a drizzle, the air pregnant with moisture. It was as if waves of energy were rolling through lifetimes and dimensions, as if something about that exact moment was changing the past and the future at the same time. He floated up higher and higher, completely free from all ties, until he passed the clouds, the atmosphere, and the moon, reflecting the galaxy in a million tiny points of light.

∞ ∞ ∞

The gunshot smashed into her dream like a rock hurled onto a frozen lake. Anna sat straight up in bed, her ears ringing, her heart beating like a kick drum. 5:55 a.m. Any second now the kids would come running in, jump into her bed, beg her to burrow down in the covers with them to hide. Then the sirens would come screaming up the hill and stop across the street at her neighbor's house where the gunshot came from. Anna breathed deeply. 5:56 a.m. Any second now her bedroom door would fling open.

Five minutes later, she still sat stiff and alone in the dark room. How could the kids not have heard that? Well, the sirens would be coming soon. There's no way the gunshot didn't wake up Mr. Johnson next door, who would've called 911 immediately. Hell, he probably had them on speed dial.

6:15 a.m. Complete silence and darkness all around, as if she was in a cocoon. She finally allowed the possibility to enter her mind that the gunshot was not at the neighbor's after all, or even in the real world. It was not a dream, of that she was sure, but where she was tapped into she had no idea. And, more importantly, why.

Anna lay back down and pulled the covers up to her chin. An owl hooted from the woods at the bottom of the hill, another answered nearby. And she drifted into a dreamless sleep, floating up and away into the lights of the Milky Way.

thirteen

"A very great vision is needed and the man who has it must follow it as the eagle seeks the deepest blue of the sky."

—Crazy Horse

March 12, 2017

Arkansas Hwy 70 East

The sun rises over soybean fields as I drive east on Highway 70 out of North Little Rock and toward Mississippi. I'll stick to the backroads, "blue highways" as my dad calls them. Makes me feel like I'm not so alone. I'm headed to Abbeville, Mississippi, where I've recently learned my grandmother Margaret was from. Even though I can't feel her with me right now, I know she is leading me there. Her ashes sit on the seat beside me in a plain wooden box.

∞ ∞ ∞

I was six years old that August. The water in the shallow end of the Pine Bluff Country Club pool was cool, not cold, soft against my skin. My mother lay under an orange umbrella, her eyes hidden behind dark sunglasses. I had no idea if they were open or closed. My brother Jacob stood in line for the diving board, and I dove under the blue water and swam to the place where the deep end started. I walked down the decline and was just about to shoot back up to the surface for air when I saw her.

Her slick, brown body was the size of an acorn cinched at the waist, and she had eight thin legs about the length of my finger. The ease with which her feet gently bounced off the bottom of the pool mesmerized me, so I tried to bounce gently to the right, just my toes touching the bottom. The spider bounced with me. I bounced left and she mirrored me, as if she was showing me how to do something I had forgotten, reminding me of something that I already knew. We continued this dance for about three minutes. Somewhere along the way it occurred to me that I was breathing underwater, but with that realization came the fact that she was, too, and that I was okay. It never occurred to me to question if it was real, doubt what I was seeing, shatter the illusion and gulp in chlorinated water. It just was, and I was, and we were.

As she turned and bounced away, I opened my mouth and filled it with water. Then I squatted and pushed off the bottom as hard as I could. I broke the surface of the pool and blew the water out like a dolphin, the sun's rays shining through the drops in rainbows.

∞ ∞ ∞

The Helena Bridge rises from the flat Delta in front of me, spanning almost a mile across the Mississippi River from West Helena, Arkansas, to Lula, Mississippi. A semi rattles the trestles and shakes my car as we pass on the narrow bridge. The Isle of Capri Casino appears on my left, sparkling on the muddy riverbank like costume jewelry.

∞ ∞ ∞

I was twelve years old when my grandmother

Margaret appeared in my dream for the first time. It was a week before she died, the last night she spent in our house before she went to the hospital and never got out. In the dream I am standing next to a large, ornate fountain on a cobblestone street. My grandmother walks up and places a small, white bone in my hands, about the size of a chicken leg, and whispers, "Remember, Anna." The bone cracks open and a cardinal steps out, red wings fluttering as he unfurls, crest pointing to the sky. The cardinal hops once and then takes flight with the bone fragments in his claws, his reflection mirroring below as he flaps over the water and drops them, the ripples spreading outward.

I had that dream every night for a week. When she died, the dream stopped. Thirty-seven years later, the dream showed up unexpectedly, knocking on the door like a long-lost friend.

∞ ∞ ∞

It's a strangely familiar sensation driving through the rolling Mississippi hills. The green is so intoxicating I can taste it on my tongue. I've never been here, yet I feel like some part of me knows the stories in the dirt. I look to my right at an enormous mound of spiraling, climbing kudzu. It takes me a minute to realize that underneath the invasive green vines is a long-abandoned house.

∞ ∞ ∞

It was 1992, a month before losing myself in a twenty-year marriage. The great redwood trees around us had kept the forest floor shaded all day from the summer sun, and the four of us had built a campfire. It flickered and glowed, casting shadows around the secluded campsite in a remote area of the forest.

This was my first visit to the ancient groves in Northern California. It was like an earlier trip to Rome; I knew I'd been there before, and I knew I'd be back. Even the smell of the mossy floor between the roots was familiar. After a campfire dinner of red snapper we had caught earlier that day and cold beer, we nestled into our tents. We were planning to get up before sunrise, and we were exhausted.

I slipped easily into sleep, the popping and crackling of the fire lulling me. The last thing I remember was thinking how soft the ground was, roots and all.

The next thing I remember is the distant sound of music. No, not music, really—singing. It was like hundreds of celestial voices singing in harmony, and I lay there letting it surround me and hold me in its embrace. I didn't open my eyes or question where it came from; I just let it envelop me. At some point the singing slowly faded and I fell back asleep.

Morning came coldly, and we packed up and hiked out to watch the sun rise over the Russian River Valley. The oranges and reds danced across the sky as we sat on the bank and drank steaming coffee. As we stood up to go, I asked the others what they thought about the singing the night before. I was sure they had heard it; it encompassed the whole grove. But they just looked at me blankly. No one had heard but me.

We drove north that afternoon to another grove. Then, two days later we headed south out of the forest on our way back to San Francisco. We passed by the grove we stayed in that first night. As we were leaving the canopy of the trees, a motel caught my eye. It was brown and rustic, and the sign hanging out front said *Singing Trees Motel.* We didn't have time to stop, but that was okay. I didn't need to.

For several miles I watched the great trees through

the back window of the car. They never disappeared, just faded into the horizon.

∞ ∞ ∞

My mother had my grandmother's ashes placed in a ceramic urn. Years later, for reasons I still don't understand, my mother insisted that I keep the urn at my house, even though I had two young daughters and a rowdy cocker spaniel. When it got knocked off the shelf and broke, my grandmother floated up into the air in a cloud of grey ash.

∞ ∞ ∞

My brother Jacob was killed two weeks ago. Last Tuesday his wife gave his ashes to me in the black plastic box they came in from the funeral home, said she couldn't afford an urn or interment. That night my grandmother appeared in my dream again after almost four decades.

The next morning I called the Christ the King Catholic Church columbarium. After the urn broke, my mother bought two niches there, one for my grandmother, one for her. My mother's interment was the first time I had seen my grandmother's name engraved on the plaque beside it.

It took two days for them to get back to me. They had never had anyone ask to remove cremains. I explained to them that I was going to take my grandmother and replace her with my brother, and I would pay for the new plaque. I could feel the nuns' eyes on me as they opened the niche and slid her out in a rectangular wooden box. The box was lighter and smaller than I had expected.

Even though it had been over ten years since she spilled in my house, I wondered if my grandmother's bones were still in the air.

∞ ∞ ∞

I turn at the "Welcome to Abbeville" sign and drive east. An old cemetery is on my right, so I pull onto the side of the road and turn off the car.

Both of our parents were only-children, so my brother and I have no aunts, uncles, or cousins. Our dad's parents died before we were born, and growing up we would only see our mother's parents once a year during Christmas. But in high school my boyfriend and I would go sit with his grandmother every Saturday at her house. Black-and-white photographs hung on walls, sat on tables, watched me from the refrigerator door. She would tell stories about her grandparents, great-grandparents, and family members in the present tense, as if they were still here. In some ways, I suppose they were. I would leave there feeling hollow, alone, as if I were standing in a huge unfurnished room.

I look out the window to the hundreds of scattered headstones. I'd never even heard the name Abbeville until I saw it on my grandmother's death certificate at the columbarium. A quick search revealed my grandmother Margaret and great-grandmother Rosemary were both from here. I knew very little about Margaret, but I'd never heard anything about Rosemary. Ever. Even though all I know now is her name, it is like learning about a whole part of myself I never even knew existed, a lifetime of stories I've never heard. It is surreal and unsettling at the same time.

I take off my shoes, open the car door, and close it behind me. The grass is soft under my feet as I walk across the graves. It's an odd sensation, as if moments are embedded in the soil, memories working their way to the surface. I walk the perimeter of the cemetery and then make my way to the middle.

In the center is a century-old oak, her branches reaching for the sky like outstretched hands. My hand touches the trunk and I leave it there as I circle around it, fingertips brushing bark.

When I get back to where I started, I feel the excitement of a new beginning, like the giddy first hour of a long road trip. But what it's the beginning of I have no idea.

I walk to my car, pull out into the road, and turn around to head back the way I came.

∞ ∞ ∞

An hour-and-a-half later the Helena Bridge appears on the horizon. The river pulls me toward her. I turn off the radio and take a deep breath, allowing the silence to envelop me. In the distance I hear the faint sound of singing, the same kind of sound from that night all those years ago in the redwood grove. And for the first time, I feel my grandmother around me like a mist.

I turn right into the casino drive and head toward the water, following the sound.

I stop at the far end of the parking lot where it turns into a gravel road that runs alongside the riverbank. A Great Blue Heron, his neck curved in an S, flaps past me and down the road, as if he is showing me the way. I roll down my window and hear the singing, a little louder now, gurgling down the river. I put my car in drive and slowly roll onto the gravel.

The river is on my left as I make my way down the road. A quarter-mile down I stop. The singing gets a little louder, so I pick up the wooden box, open my door, and step out of the car barefoot.

A short trail leads between trees to the riverbank. At the end it opens up to a small beach. The brown water laps the shore, and I feel like I am between worlds as I set the wooden box on the sand and then step to the shoreline and the water brushes over my feet. The singing is now rising from the water like wisps of smoke, lulling me to close my eyes, hundreds and hundreds of female voices singing in harmony that run up through my soles and back out through my fingertips. I hear my grandmother's voice behind me join in, and I know it's time.

I pick up the box, unhinge the latch, and walk into the river ankle-deep. I turn the box over and my grandmother's bones are picked up by the wind and take flight, scattering on top of the water like a dusting of snow.

The brown water swirls in spirals. Something moves beside me. I look over to see a red snake slithering down the sand and out on top of the water. Then, just a few yards in front of me, a fish jumps, silver scales shining in the sunlight. Right as it splashes back in the water another fish jumps, and then another, until hundreds of fish are glittering in the sunlight like stars. I hear my mother's voice join in the singing, and for the first time I feel connected to a family I've never known, something bigger than the universe yet smaller than a cell at the same time.

And I close my eyes, take a deep breath, and begin to sing.

∞ ∞ ∞

The moonlight shines through my bedroom window as I place the tip of my pen on the paper, the ink a tiny black spot on the white, and pause. The girls are at their dad's, the dog is asleep, and I can feel stories breathing in the air around me.

I look to the window just as a hummingbird darts through it as if the glass wasn't there, hovers in front of me, and then swoops down and dives through the end of my pen. The pen strokes are fluid as I write the first name: *Talako.* Three more hummingbirds follow, three more names. *Hashilli*, *Hushushi*, *Onnat Minti.*

I sit back and look at the paper. Instinctively I know they are names, but I have no idea whose or even what language. The names begin vibrating, as if they are creating a frequency that is just out of my range, a sound I know down in the spirals of my DNA but had forgotten. I close my eyes and let the vibration enter me and then pulse outwards in waves.

When the waves reach the stars and then echo back to me, I open my eyes. The air is still yet pregnant, like the air before a storm. "What do I do?" I ask aloud as I place the tip of my pen back on the blank page.

Begin, they whisper.

Begin.

"But, as an ideal, we live and will live, not only in the splendor of our past, the poetry of our legends and art, not only in the interfusion of our blood with yours, and in our faithful adherence to the ideals of American citizenship, but in the living heart of the nation."

—Ohiyesa

Author's Note

This book is a work of historical fiction.

The Treaty at Dancing Rabbit Creek (1830) and the tragedy at the Arkansas Post (1831), however, are very real.

For two weeks in December of 1831, after the signing of the Treaty at Dancing Rabbit Creek, the first removal treaty carried into effect under President Andrew Jackson's Indian Removal Act, over 2000 Choctaw, who ferried down the Mississippi River from Memphis, Tennessee or up from Vicksburg, Mississippi, were stranded at the Arkansas Post when their steamboats were dispatched to Fort Smith. Then, the Arkansas River froze. While the numbers vary, hundreds of men, women, and children, many of whom were barefoot, died of starvation and exposure in that two-week period. There are no marked graves, no plaque describing the tragedy, and no record of where they were buried.

Most people have never heard of this. I had not, and neither had my ex-husband or any of his family, even though he grew up less than a quarter mile from the exact spot and spent many hours playing there.

The *Reindeer* survivors were then forced to walk to present-day North Little Rock before they continued walking to Indian Territory. According to several sources, upon arrival in Little Rock, a Choctaw chief was asked by a reporter from the *Arkansas Gazette* how the removals were going. His response, that so far it had been a "trail of tears and death," was picked up by the Eastern press and forever forged in our shared memory.

By 1835, 30,000 Choctaw had been forcibly removed from their ancestral land in Mississippi. Thousands did not survive. Those who chose to stay in Mississippi were harassed and even murdered, and most had to go into hiding.

During the Cherokee removals in the mid-to-late 1830's, again people were forced to leave their ancestral homeland. Those who hid out in the remote mountains of North Carolina would later become the Eastern Band of Cherokee Indians, whose descendants are still living there today.

Native Americans were not granted citizenship until 1924, six years after the Choctaw and Cherokee code talkers perplexed the Germans in World War I, turning it around for the Americans. At the same time, Indian children back home were being beaten in school for speaking in their native language. These brave Choctaw and Cherokee soldiers paved the way for the better-known Navajo code talkers in World War II.

∞ ∞ ∞

As a nation, we must remember our past, all of it, so that we can learn from it and each other. We must look beyond what we're taught in history books and open ourselves up to the stories still living in the soil, the trees, and the water. And we must relearn how to listen, truly listen.

This novel started in the summer of 2016 in the mountains of western North Carolina when my grandmother, who died in 1992, came to me and asked me to listen. While I felt very close to her as a child, I knew virtually nothing about her. I hadn't felt her presence at all for almost twenty-five years. I admit, I resisted writing this book at first. But the more I got out of my own way, the more the stories, and the storytellers, appeared, both literally and figuratively.

I traveled throughout Arkansas, Mississippi, Oklahoma, Tennessee, Georgia, and North Carolina, spending hours upon hours hiking in mossy national forests, wandering across rich delta farmland, walking barefoot through forgotten cemeteries, sitting beside ancient, singing rivers. And listening, just listening. If I have not been true to the story it's my fault, not theirs.

I hope that I have made them proud.

Selected Sources

Gibson, Arrell Morgan, and George Lynn Cross. "America's Exiles: Indian Colonization in Oklahoma." *The Gateway to Oklahoma History*. Retrieved from http://gateway.okhistory.org/ark:/67531/metadc862891/m1/5, Accessed August 11, 2016.

Greenwood, Lee. "Trail of Tears from Mississippi Walked by our Ancestors." *Choctaw Nation Bishinik*, March 1995.

"History and Legacy of Cherokee Code Talkers Sought." *Cherokee Nation News Release.* November 15, 2010. Retrieved from www.cherokee.org/News/Stories/32170, Accessed January 03, 2017.

Horne, Amber M. "The Choctaw: Footprints Across Arkansas: Trail of Tears Removal Corridors for the Cherokees, Chickasaws, Choctaws, Creeks & Seminoles." *Indian Removal Routes in Arkansas.* Arkansas Historic Preservation Program. Retrieved from www.arkansaspreservation.com/Preservation-Services/indian-removal-routes-in-arkansas, Accessed August 10, 2016.

Nerburn, Kent, Ed. *The Wisdom of the Native Americans.* MJF Books, New York: 1999.

Paige, Amanda L., Fuller L. Bumpers, and Daniel F. Littlefield, Jr. "Coleman Creek Trail of Tears Park on the Choctaw and Chickasaw Trail of Tears:

Historical Contexts Reports." UALR Site Report, Part IV. *Trail of Tears Through Arkansas.* Retrieved from Sequoyah National Research Center, www.ualrexhibits.org/trailoftears/places/ualr-site-report-part4, Accessed November 01, 2016.

Paige, Amanda L., Fuller L. Bumpers, and Daniel F. Littlefield, Jr. "Little Rock and Choctaw Removal." Little Rock Site Report, Page 2. *Trail of Tears Through Arkansas.* Retrieved from Sequoyah National Research Center, www.ualrexhibits.org/trailoftears/places/little-rock-site-report-page-2, Accessed November 01, 2016.

Paige, Amanda L., Fuller L. Bumpers, and Daniel F. Littlefield, Jr. "North Little Rock Site on the Trail of Tears National Historic Trail: Historical Contexts Report, 2003." American Native Press Archives. University of Arkansas at Little Rock. Retrieved from National Park Service, www.nps.gov/trte/learn/historyculture/arkansas.htm, Accessed October 09, 2016.

Winterman, Denise. "World War One: The Original Code Talkers." *BBC News Magazine.* May 19, 2014. Retrieved from www.bbc.com/news/magazine-26963624, Accessed January 03, 2017.

Wright, Muriel H. "The Removal of the Choctaws to the Indian Territory, 1830-1833." *Chronicles of Oklahoma*, Volume 6, No. 2. June, 1928: 103-128.

Acknowledgments

I am so thankful for my friends and family who made me feel supported and loved as I dove headfirst into the writing of this book: Mom for your love and help piecing together the past from fragments; Dad for your unwavering support; and Caren and Tacey for reading early drafts and witnessing with grace. I'm eternally grateful for Bloom for helping me step into my power, for Paula's beautiful words and encouragement, and for Laurie, Gretchen, Kandy, Donna, Diane, and Amy for reading, listening, and making me feel not quite so crazy. And for my children, Annaliese, Sophia, and Jude, who helped me to truly understand that if we can gather our courage and heal ourselves, we then heal those who came before, and those who come after.

About the Author

Paula Martin was born in Pine Bluff, Arkansas and spent her formative years in Little Rock. She received her MFA in creative writing from the University of New Orleans before going on to create and produce the internationally-syndicated *Tales from the South* radio show. A recipient of the Arkansas Arts Council Governor's Arts Award, and the 2017 Inductee into the Arkansas Writers' Hall of Fame, Paula lives in Little Rock with her three children.

CPSIA information can be obtained
at www.ICGtesting.com
Printed in the USA
BVOW11s2049210917
495457BV00022B/947/P

9 780984 619993